When Murder Gilds the Skies

By Tammy Cullers

REDBIRD PUBLISHING

Copyright © 2024 by Tammy Cullers
ISBN 979-8-9911513-0-6 (paperback)
ISBN 979-8-9911513-1-3 (ebook)
Library of Congress Control Number: 2024914979

Printed in the United States of America
Cover design: Tammy F. Cullers

This is a work of fiction. Names, characters, places, and incidents either
are the product of the author's imagination. Any resemblance to actual
persons, living or dead is entirely coincidental.

For Randall

Chapter 1

The Rev. Jane Cartwright spotted the needle on her speedometer at the same time she noticed the swirling blue lights in her rearview mirror. No matter how fast she drove on the freeway, Rick, her late husband, always claimed if she ever received a speeding ticket, it would be for driving forty in a twenty-five-mile-an-hour zone. He wasn't wrong. She pulled over to the side of the road and watched the lanky police officer tuck his clipboard under his arm and walk toward her car.

"Good evening, ma'am. I'm Officer Orie Smith with the Crooked Run Police Department. Do you know why I pulled you over this evening?"

"Oh, uh, hello, Officer. I didn't realize I was going so fast. Was I speeding?"

"Yes, ma'am. I clocked you at 20 miles over the legal limit. May I please see your driver's license and registration?"

Jane leaned over and pulled the vehicle registration from a stack of papers in the glove compartment.

"Thank you. Hmmm. Reverend Jane Cartwright. I see you haven't gotten around to changing your address. Pasadena, California? That's a long way from the Shenandoah Valley."

Jane nodded. She'd come a long way on many levels. "Yes. I need to make a trip to the DMV and get that changed. I have thirty days, right?"

"Yes, ma'am. But make sure you get it done." He pulled his wire-rimmed glasses down the bridge of his nose and looked down at her as though he were a professor calling out a neglectful student. "Stay in your vehicle while I check out your paperwork."

Where does he think I'd go? Jane wondered, twisting a graying curl around her finger. She sighed. One more reason for the folks of Crooked Run to wish she had never come to their town. She imagined Deacon Reginald Reynolds now, head reared back, thumbs hooked into his belt loops, a trickle of tobacco staining the crease between the corner of his mouth and jaw. "It's what happens when you hire a woman to do a man's job. Endangering lives and misguiding souls."

She gazed out the window at the town she'd recently claimed as her home. A tumbleweed toppled down the street and stopped in front of her new place of service: Crooked Run Fellowship. The church's siding was weathered and rough and needed painting. A large, empty bell tower stood where the steeple might have been, and the iron railing next to the steep concrete steps was rusty with age. But someone had neatly trimmed the boxwoods along the path to the door, and the stained glass windows sparkled with a glossy shine.

A tap on her window brought her back to reality.

"Ma'am, I've checked your information, and everything appears to be in order. However, I do need to inform you that speeding is dangerous and against the law. Is there a reason you were in such a hurry?"

"No, I'm on the way to choir practice. I'm afraid I wasn't focusing on driving like I should have been."

"I understand. These things happen, but we set speed limits for a reason. I'll need to issue you a citation for speeding this evening. You can pay the fine within 30 days or contest it in court." His voice slipped into a monotone, and Jane knew he'd said those exact words a thousand times before.

"Thank you, officer. I will pay more attention to my driving next time." She crossed her fingers and prayed he wouldn't connect her name to the new assistant pastor at Crooked Run Fellowship. All hope of anonymity vanished with his following words.

"Rev. Cartwright. Fancy, we should meet like this. I look forward to hearing you speak. I had to miss the past two weeks, but I plan to be at church on Sunday."

Jane blushed. "I'd hoped you didn't recognize me. I don't suppose I made a favorable first impression."

He snapped his clipboard shut and lowered his voice. "We all make mistakes, Rev. It would be good for you to remember that."

"Wise words, officer. I will keep them in mind."

She rolled up her window and merged back out into the traffic. Perhaps she should buy a bicycle and ride around town like G.K. Chesterton's Father Brown. Perhaps she should take the next plane to anywhere.

***

"I'm sorry, but I can't make it to choir practice this evening, Vada." Lillie Fairchild settled into the recliner and unfolded the footrest. Strands of wispy gray tendrils came loose from the elastic band around her hair, and beads of sweat stood out on her forehead. "I'm exhausted," she groaned. "Getting Emily's room ready is all I can handle in one day." She leaned into the comfy chair and closed her eyes. Her pink wool sweater and fuzzy black skirt made her look like a needle-felted doll.

"Oh, don't whine, Lillie. I worked twice as hard as you and am not too tired to sing. Vada was two years older than her sister, but newcomers to Crooked Run still believed they were twins—two plump, rosy-cheeked matrons. "I washed the windows, shampooed the rug, and hung up new blinds. And what did you do? You painted a four-foot square of canvas." Vada grabbed an insert from a stack of newspapers on the floor beside her and fanned her flushed face. Charcoal, the family cat, took advantage of an open lap and hopped up for an evening snooze.

"Oh, but the mental strain, Vada. You don't understand what it's like to be an artist. Painting that 'square of canvas,' as you call it, took more emotional energy than all your cleaning put together. I had to blend the colors to create the perfect shade, sketch the shape, and, the most arduous task of all, fit it into the frame." Lillie pulled a faded quilt over her legs and snuggled farther into the recliner. "I can't handle any more emotion this evening. You know what Clarence is like when we practice for the choir competition."

"You don't have a choice, Lillie. You're our loudest alto. Edith Black can't find the pitch without you. Clarence says she sounds like a dobro sliding into her note! Besides, Emily won't come until Friday, so you'll have another day to rest. All we have to do is stay on key, and Clarence won't yell. He only wants us to sound our best."

6

Lillie pursed her lips. "You take his side every time. Just let a single man come into town, and you forget your age and your blood relation and simper like a teenager."

"Are you serious, Lillie? We're both in our seventies. I don't have the slightest remembrance of what it's like to be a teenager. Now, let's change out of these filthy clothes and grab a bite to eat. We can leave at 6:20 and still make it to church on time."

"I wonder if the new Rev. will be at practice? I haven't decided what I think about a woman preacher." Lillie, an artist, prided herself on her open mind, but females in religious leadership were a conundrum. She didn't like anybody telling her how to behave — especially another woman.

"You and half of the rest of the congregation. I'm surprised Rev. Cartwright got the votes she needed to win the majority."

Lillie shook her head. "Reggie said she won by only 12 votes."

"He discussed private church business with you?" Vada's voice raised an octave. "He's not supposed to share that kind of information. Votes are confidential!"

"He didn't say who voted for her and who didn't, Vada." Lillie snorted. "Besides, she's an assistant, not a full-time minister."

"Rev. Barnard has talked about retiring for the past five years. I bet he won't be around another six months since Rev. Cartwright is here to take his place. Still, deacons shouldn't discuss such matters with regular church members. Now, you should change your clothes and get ready for choir practice." Vada stood, and Charcoal slid to the floor, meowing her displeasure at being dumped.

Lillie sighed. "I guess I can summon the energy. We'll have to limit our evenings out when our sister Emily moves back."

"What do you mean? We don't go out much, and I suspect Emily will want to join the choir too."

"You truly believe they will let a murderer sing in the church choir? I've got my doubts." Lillie pushed down the footrest with a bang and stood up. "If I'm not mistaken, killing people breaks one or two of the Ten Commandments."

***

Mayor Marcus Justice signed his name on the last document from the pile of forms his secretary, Sara Floyd, left on his desk.

He detested paperwork more than anything else in his job. And now, he had twice as much as the town manager just left for vacation.

He stretched his legs under the sleek metal desk and ran his hand through his thick salt and pepper hair. Many of his friends had already turned gray. Some had lost most of their hair. He might be almost sixty-five, but his mind was still in its thirties. Years of intentional, health-conscious living paid off. Bean sprouts and tofu. An occasional yoga class. Many people didn't want to sacrifice calorie-laden food to be healthy. He had never tasted a deep-fat fried oyster that satisfied as much as an admiring glance from a female. Once in a while, an occasional ache in his left knee reminded him that, sometime–way in the distant future, age would catch up with him. But that day was far away.

Today had been a humdinger. The town manager hadn't even made it to the airport to leave for his Bahama cruise when the Main Street water line cracked. Water poured out into streets and yards, flooding drains and low-lying fields. It splashed into the feed mill's backyard and ruined a truckload of straw they stacked in the pole shed that morning. The utility workers had to turn off the water for the entire town for four hours while they replaced the pipes.

As a temporary town manager, Marcus called in the maintenance crew and oversaw the cleanup. Thankfully, Sara had dealt with most of the complaints and calls. The citizens of Crooked Run believed he should be able to snap his fingers and, like Mary Poppins, put everything in order again. Nobody had patience anymore.

And then, to top it all off, Olive Thomas, the town gossip, thought she caught sight of a rabid skunk in her back garden. She'd called every emergency number she had loaded on speed dial. Within five minutes, they all gathered on her lawn only to find her neighbor's cat, Stripe, snoozing among the dried cornstalks. To be fair, the feline resembled a skunk in the right light. In the meantime, at least four stories circulated throughout the town speculating about the events at Thomas's place. Of course, that meant more calls to the town office. Sara deserved a bonus for putting up with all the drama.

And now he had to go to choir practice. Once, he found joy in singing with the Harmony choir at the Crooked Run Fellowship. He had a powerful bass voice (or so he'd been told) and led the men's section in most anthems. But things changed when Clarence Jackson came to town. The man was a social climber. He hadn't been in Crooked Run for two weeks when he situated himself in the back row of the church choir. He sang too loud and made snide remarks about pitch and tone to men who had been part of the choir for decades.

The same day their previous choir director announced retirement, Clarence rushed to Rev. Barnard and volunteered to step into the position. He said he'd studied music at Julliard. That distinction alone charmed Rev. Barnard and impressed most of the old ladies. Clarence emitted sweetness and light until he stood behind the director's podium. As soon as he raised his arms to lead, his Jeckyl became Hyde. Marcus wondered if the new assistant pastor, Rev. Jane Cartwright, would have been as susceptible to Clarence's charm as the Rev. Bernard.

Marcus hadn't voted for Cartwright. Although he didn't have a problem with females in the clergy, he preferred not to have a woman lead his church. Women, in his view, were too tentative. People needed somebody who would tell them how to behave. He liked decisiveness and power. He sometimes pictured himself playing the character of Moses in The Ten Commandments. Move over, Charlton Heston. He'd broken his share of the ten rules for respectabe living. But in his opinion, commandments were like grammar rules—once you knew them, you could break them.

Marcus closed the cover on his laptop and stood up to leave. Cinda, his wife, was visiting her mother in Raleigh. She'd most likely be gone another two weeks. He didn't mind living the bachelor's life while she was gone. He felt refreshed by the change. Besides, Cinda had started asking too many questions about his business life. Nothing annoyed him more than explaining corporate intricacies to a travel agent.

She and her mother were two peas in a pod. He preferred Cinda travel to North Carolina rather than having her mother visit them. He didn't think he could stand them both in the house at the same time. According to Cinda's mom, he dressed too young, used too much hair gel, and ate like a yoga instructor.

The chimes on the bell tower reminded him of the hour. Six o'clock. He'd have to move faster to make it to choir practice on time. His final business task of the night would have to wait. He hated to put it off again, but everything had to be done in order. This project allowed no room for error. None.

***

"You're not taking your electric guitar to church tonight, are you, Brayden?" His mother, Sara Floyd, set a plate of egg rolls and a dish of lo mein on the coffee table. She could always count on The Asian Express for tasty food at an affordable price. She never had time to cook on choir practice nights.

"You've gotta be kidding, Mom! Not take my Gibson? It can play rings around any other instrument in the church!" Brayden grinned. He loved to see the envy in his buddy's eyes when he pulled baby G. out of the case.

"Brayden, you know how Clarence dislikes the sound of electric guitars. Can't you and the boys practice on a different night?"

Brayden took an egg roll and peeled away the wrapper. "Do you really want to drive me into town another night? The other guys likely wouldn't be able to find rides, and they couldn't all fit in our Jeep. Besides, who would

9

supervise CJ's precious equipment? We wouldn't use his crappy stuff if it were the last soundboard on Earth, but try to make him believe that. He thinks we're planning to blow the fuses on those two old amps he puts on the stage every week."

"Be respectful, Brayden," his mom said. "He did study at Julliard, you know."

"He thinks he has the right to dis our arrangements because he went to a moldy old music school. He's about two hundred years behind the times. Besides, we won't disturb his precious practice. Carter's gonna bring his portable sound system. All we need is space."

"Well, make sure you don't interrupt the choir rehearsal. Our big competition will be here in a few weeks. Practice is getting pretty intense."

He nodded. "We don't need to go into the sanctuary. Carter's cheap Bluetooth is better than anything you all have on your soundboard. They need to replace all of that stuff. It's gonna blow up someday."

"We manage fine with our outdated equipment," his mom said. "The voices make the melodies, not some expensive gadget."

Brayden shook his head. "You just go on thinking that, mom. The wiring is so old we blow a fuse every time we hook up more than two instruments. Plus, we have to use an adapter for every plug because all the electrical outlets only have two prongs."

Her eyes wandered to the expensive guitar propped beside her son's chair. Her ex-in-laws could have bought the instrument with pocket change. However, when her former husband Chris left, the relatives also vanished. She could understand why they might not want to stay in contact with her, but she couldn't fathom how they could ghost their only grandchild. The guitar seemed to mock her as the sunlight reflected off the silver bridge. Thank God Brayden didn't know the true price she had paid for that sleek instrument.

    ***

Dave Harper, the sound technician at Crooked Run Fellowship, wiped his hands on his jeans and unscrewed the back of the amplifier. He was almost sure the "sound crisis" described by Clarence Jackson would be nothing more than a blown fuse or a dirty jack. He traced the circuit wires with his fingers, tugging on them to make sure none were loose. No slack there. He inspected the fuses, and all was clear with them as well. He positioned his voltmeter probe after the first resistor in the signal chain to verify its proper operation. The meter read zero—an easy fix.

A slight ping came from somewhere in the sanctuary, and Dave hoped the high and mighty choir director had not come in early to supervise his work. Clarence's whining voice was the last thing he wanted to hear.

With the soldering iron in hand, he knelt next to the amp. With any luck, nobody would notice him.

Dave had almost quit his sound job when Clarence took over as choir director. It wasn't an actual job, just an opportunity to get out of the house. His dad needed him more and more each day, and that fact both scared him and made him feel trapped. And that feeling of being trapped always carried a burden of guilt. His dad sacrificed a lot for Dave and his brother when they were kids. It must have been tough for him, being a single parent to two energetic boys. Dave's mom had died the month after his little brother turned three. His dad worked two jobs to keep the family in food and clothes.

However, since the tractor accident six months ago, his dad had depended entirely on others to help him get through his daily routine.

He thought his dad would have shown some improvement by now. The doctor warned that healing would take time, but Dave underestimated how long it would actually take. Meanwhile, their money was running low. He hoped the side gig he'd picked up would be worth the trouble. Because it was trouble—a lot of trouble.

***

Clarence Jackson adjusted his bowtie and stood up straight. He might be 66, but women still found him attractive. When he first came to Crooked Run, it amused him to hear some of the church ladies giggle as he walked past. That hair-growing salve he bought from an online ad worked well. At first, he doubted it would be effective. Scammers got more wily by the moment. But he could tell his curly white hair had more volume than last month. The 39 dollars he shelled out for the product was money well spent. And since lack of money was no longer an issue, he could afford to buy the salve for years to come. He winked at his reflection.

Clarence was eager for practice this evening. He hoped Lillie Fairchild would show up. Lillie's personality could sometimes be flaky, but she sang a decent alto. She didn't have a perfect pitch but came close enough for a church choir. Mayor Marcus's voice didn't have the timbre for lead bass, but he hit most of the notes, and that was as much as Clarence could hope for. His friend and fellow musician, Professor Carina Vincent, agreed to stop by rehearsal soon and give suggestions to the group. He hoped to have them in near-perfect form by then.

The anthem was progressing well. Clarence believed the Harmony Choir at Crooked Run Fellowship would impress the judges with their exceptional performance. Maybe they'd win first place; it wasn't out of the question. He'd have to make sure his passport was up to date. First place meant a two-week tour of Europe's greatest cathedrals. Going to Europe with unlimited cash would be a novel experience for him.

Ave Maria wasn't his first choice for the performance. But he had to be realistic. He'd been leading the choir for only a few months. The singers would be ready for more complex music next year. He would shape and mold their minor talents to perfection. Yes, his move back to Crooked Run was paying off well. Many pieces of his plan had already fallen into place.

A jingle from his doorbell pulled him out of his reverie. Who could that be? No matter who skulked about his house at this hour, he'd get rid of them. He didn't want to set a poor example by being late for choir rehearsal this evening.

To his surprise, no one stood outside when he opened the door. He glanced around the street but spotted nobody. Puzzled, he started to close the door when he detected a yellow envelope on the stoop. Although the front of the envelope didn't have a name or an address, he knew someone meant it for him. He pried the sticky glue from the flap and pulled out a sheet of white printer paper. Bright red cut-out letters shouted at him: "Prepare to meet thy God."

Chapter 2

Jane pulled her Toyota pickup into the Crooked Run Fellowship parking lot and let the motor idle. Her brief run-in with Officer Smith put her behind schedule, but she lingered in her car. She watched Sara Floyd drop off several teenage boys at the church basement door. Each one carried a music case and appeared eager to start practice. Sara was a saint. She didn't know how the young woman coped as a single parent. Although Jane didn't have children of her own, she imagined raising a sixteen-year-old boy alone was not for the faint of heart. Not to mention the financial burden. Despite everything, Sara remained cheerful, and Brayden was well-adjusted.

Jane scolded herself for being a coward. Sara, the courageous super-mom, faced the daunting choir director head-on, while Jane, a seasoned pastoral caregiver, stayed in her car to avoid dealing with the man. Jane loved to sing and enjoyed her role in the choir. However, she did not enjoy their choir director's pompous attitude. But she was five minutes late already. She had to face the music. Smiling at her unintentional idiom, she patted her rebellious hair into place and opened the car door.

The church stood across the street from the Crooked Run Community Park. The entire field glinted bronze in the sunset—postcard perfection. Suddenly, a slight movement caught her eye. A man stood at the park's entrance. His shabby jacket and muddy jeans contrasted with the crisp beauty of the evening. He held a walking stick, and beside him lay a ragged backpack. Who was he? And why did he stare so intently at the Crooked Run Fellowship Church? She shivered and quickened her pace toward the church door.

Clarence appeared in fine form as Jane slipped into her seat in the soprano section. His waving arms and jiggling bowtie reminded her of a cartoon figure–a caricature of himself. Why so animated? And why a bowtie at a weeknight practice? Would this man's vanity never end? She nodded at Vada Fairchild and joined the warm-up song - When Morning Guilds the Skies. The hymn was one of Clarence's favorites. Jane was surprised he hadn't arranged that song for the choir competition instead of the more difficult Ave Maria.

"Find the pitch! Get on top of that F sharp, or it will go flat!" Clarence lowered his hands to the floor to represent the level to which the melody would descend if they didn't steer it in the right direction. "Alto section. Don't slide into those notes. Hit them sharp from the start."

"I'm doing my best." Edith looked pointedly at the empty chair beside her. "I need to pick out Lillie's note to find my pitch."

"As you can see," Clarence snapped, "Lillie is not here. I hope she is running late and not skipping out on us. Our illustrious mayor is not here, either. Maybe they don't consider it important to rehearse our anthem only weeks before the state competition. Perhaps they have already reached the state of perfection."

"A lot happened at the office today," said Sara. "The mayor will be here in a while. He still had some loose ends to tie up when I left."

"Trinity church choir will practice tonight." Clarence continued as if Sara hadn't spoken. "And I can assure you that every member is present without excuses. I talked with their director, Bethel Green, yesterday, and she is confident they will win the grand prize this year. She's making sure each choir member has a passport."

"That's right," said the Harmony Choir pianist Anne Farmer. "First prize is a tour of European cathedrals!" She glanced around the old sanctuary and sighed. "I'd be happy if we could just fix the roof here at Crooked Run Fellowship."

"What is the Trinity Choir singing for the contest?" asked Jen Crim, a timid young soprano.

Clarence stared at her in disbelief, and she appeared to wilt before him. "Why in the world do you think she'd tell me? We're in a competition, Jen, not a friendly music jam. She wouldn't risk our choir sabotaging their music."

"No need to be sarcastic, Clarence," came a voice from the back row. Deputy Brad Harris had come straight from work and wore his official Crooked Run Police uniform. "And anyway, how would it be possible for us to sabotage a musical arrangement?" Brad continued. "We turned the song lists into the state awards committee last week. Anybody can find them on the website."

Clarence scowled, but before he could respond, the back door of the sanctuary swung open. It carried in a rush of cold air and the scurrying figures of Vada and Lillie Fairchild, followed by mayor, Marcus Justice.

"So sorry," panted Lillie. "That light at the bottom of Main Street was stuck on yellow, and we couldn't drive through."

"What do you mean 'you couldn't drive through'?" growled Clarence. "Yellow means to clear the intersection, not sit there and wait for it to change to red."

"You think I don't know that?" Lillie said as she unwrapped a long scarf that appeared to encircle her entire body. "I've lived in this town decades longer than you have. I didn't want it to turn red the moment I tried to drive through. Running a red light wouldn't reflect very well on our reputation, what with Emily coming...." Her voice trailed off.

"I am unaware of the connection between going through a yellow light and Emily–whomever she may be. But enough nonsense. Hurry into your places, ladies. We'll go over our warm-up song again since we have our lead soprano and alto here."

Murmurs arose from the soprano section. The verdict on Vada's voice was still out. Although her tone was sharp, she exaggerated the vibrato, turning a simple melody into an opera aria.

If Clarence had made the rules, he'd have enlisted a pair of elementary school boys to hit the high notes. Children's voices were pure and clear. Not to mention, young people were easier to mold into shape than adults. But the contest had its requirements. Participants must be at least eighteen to enter, so Vada it was.

"Now," said Clarence, facing the choir. He placed both hands on the podium as if squeezing the hard metal would keep his ire in check. "As you can tell, we still have a way to go before we're ready for the competition. The problem is we have so little time to practice. So, we will increase our rehearsal schedule. Plan to add Saturdays to our practice schedule for the

15

next two weeks."

A collective groan rippled through the risers.

"But the youth group plans to perform their concert Saturday night," said Sara Floyd with a worried glance. "They've practiced the music for six weeks. They're already handing out flyers."

Clarence scowled. "Yes, I've heard the racket in the basement. But no matter. They'll have to reschedule. Our practice time is the top priority. They can bang on those overpriced instruments another day."

"But…" Sara protested, but Clarence cut her off.

"Now choir, stand up straight, shoulders back, relax, and smile! It's time to start our anthem." He waved his arms as he set the tempo, and Anne banged out the introduction.

"Stop!" Clarence shouted. "Anne! We've gone over this a hundred times! Ava Maria is not swing. It's not jazz. It's religious worship. Try it again, and don't be so free with the rhythm this time."

But before Anne could play a single chord, a loud groan came from above. Nails shrieked as the old wooden boards were wrenched from the ceiling. Seconds later, one of the enormous speakers crashed to the ground, the hard wooden base mere inches from the director's stand.

It happened so fast that none of the choir members had time to react. They stood in horror as Clarence dropped to the floor, hands above his head. Miraculously, the speaker did not hit him full-on. A stray piece of drywall grazed his forehead and tore the skin above his eyes. Blood dripped down his nose and onto the floor.

Someone in the front row screamed, and Mayor Marcus rushed over to Clarence with a look of horror.

"What happened, man? Are you okay? I knew they shouldn't have installed those enormous speakers. They were too heavy for that old plaster ceiling! Somebody call 911! Get him some water!"

Jane had already called the emergency number, and Vada dabbed at the cut on Clarence's head with a dainty embroidered handkerchief. Anne handed him a styrofoam cup of water. He took a long drink and motioned for the ladies to step aside. Dazed, Clarence rose and brushed the drywall off his pants. He surveyed the debris beside him and then looked up at the gaping hole in the ceiling.

The wail of sirens came near, and blue and red lights reflected off the stained glass windows.

Several more chunks of plaster fell as the back double doors opened and emergency responders wheeled a stretcher inside.

"Everybody stand back," shouted a man dressed in green Crooked Run emergency squad coveralls. "More of the ceiling might come down."

The group crowded around Clarence. Two paramedics walked him to the front pew and lowered him to a sitting position. "Can you tell us what happened?" one of them asked. Clarence shook his head, still gazing at the split drywall. Electric wires dangled from the torn patches and faded pink insulation puffed out like timeworn cotton candy.

"Let him find his bearings, then we'll see if we can load him onto the gurney," said another first responder. "He's in shock. Doc needs to have a look at that cut."

The mayor stood up and took charge once more. "Folks, rehearsal is over for the night. Go home and rest. We can't practice without a leader. We'll be in touch."

"What about the mess?" asked Deputy Harris.

Marcus kicked a chunk of plaster away from the altar. "It's too late to clean it up tonight. I'll call Petrel Claims first thing in the morning. The ceiling and roof are long overdue for replacement. If we're lucky, the insurance settlement will pay for most of the repairs. For now, we can't allow anyone in the sanctuary. It's a safety hazard."

Jane nodded. "Somebody ought to call the properties chair, though. It's late, but I'm sure he'd like to know about the ceiling damage."

"I'll bring Norm up to speed on the way home. Again, there isn't anything we can do tonight."

"Thanks. I'll contact Rev. Barnard and let him know what happened."

Marcus nodded. "We'll also need to find another place to practice. We won't be able to use the sanctuary for the next day or so, but Clarence will want to keep up the rehearsal schedule once he calms down. Nothing as trivial as a near-death experience will deter him from a shot at a first-place trophy."

Deputy Harris wandered over to stand beside Jane and Marcus. "I bet we'd be able to use the town recreation center. There are a few smaller rooms off to the side of the game room. Clarence might not like the acoustics, but practicing at the rec center is better than no practice."

"I assume they have a piano?" asked Jane.

"Yes, they have one in the room the senior center uses. I can have my mom ask tomorrow when she goes over to play bingo."

"I'll set it up, Brad," said Marcus. "Don't bother your mom. It's on my way."

Just like Marcus to take charge, thought Jane. Rev. Barnard depended on him to lead several church committees, but she hadn't worked with him on any projects yet. A steady stream of Marcus might not be as bad as a steady stream of Clarence. But it would soon take its toll on her nerves.

"Thank you," said Jane. "Keep me updated."

Marcus nodded. "Looks like Clarence got his speech back."

Jane glanced over to the front row of pews, where their choir director shouted at a paramedic.

"No, I don't need to see a doctor. I'm fine. If you want to be useful, take my wool jacket to the dry cleaners." He jabbed his finger at the plaster-covered garment.

"We're sorry, sir. But if you decline medical treatment, you need to sign this form," said one of the uniformed men. He handed Clarence a clipboard and a pen.

Clarence glared at the man, but he scribbled his name on the dotted line. His legs wobbled as he stood up, but his voice didn't waver. "I've had enough excitement for one evening. I'm going home."

"Let me drive you," said Jane. "You've had a shock, and your forehead is still bleeding. You can come back for your car tomorrow."

Clarence shook his head. "I'm alright. Nothing a bit of rest can't remedy." He shuffled to the back of the church, holding on to the pews for support.

The other choir members took Clarence's lead and filed out the back door.

Jane sat in her car, still stunned by the evening's events. As she put the keys in the ignition, she spotted Dave Harper coming out the front door. On impulse, she got out of her vehicle and waved him over.

"Are you doing okay, Dave? It's been quite a night. A bit more dramatic than usual."

He nodded. "More than I bargained for, that's for sure."

"What do you think caused it?" she asked. "The speaker falling, I mean."

The wind had picked up from the north, and Dave shifted from foot to foot as he tried to stay warm. "Old ceilings and heavy speakers. Those two don't work together. I told Marcus we were taking a dangerous chance when he had me install those monsters."

"Marcus wanted them installed?" Jane narrowed her eyes. "That's strange. He made it sound like he was against attaching the speakers to the old wooden beams."

Dave tilted his head back in surprise. "That's not true. I was with him when he bought them. He said we could find a solid joist to hang them from."

"How curious. Still, I don't suppose the speaker would have to weigh much to cause injury falling from such a distance." Jane pulled her coat tight around her. October was showing its frigid side.

"You're right," Dave said. "Clarence is lucky the speaker didn't hit him."

"I hope he's okay. He should have gone to the hospital."

"Yeah, probably."

"I'll drop by his house on the way home and check on him."

"Better you than me," said Dave.

Jane smiled. "It's part of my pastoral duties. By the way, how's your dad? I need to visit him soon."

Dave shrugged. "Okay, I guess. I wish he'd try a little harder, though."

"What do you mean?"

"Some days, I think Dad's given up trying to get any better. The doctor thinks it's possible he could recover the feeling in his legs, but Dad doesn't believe him. He's too depressed to see any hope."

"He's in a tough situation. I'll make it a point to stop by your house this week."

"Thanks, Rev. Cartwright."

"Just Jane," she smiled. "We're fellow choir members, after all."

"Oh, Dave! There you are!" Anne Farmer hurried toward them. "Hi, Jane. Mind if I borrow Dave for a few minutes? I'm worried the roof might leak since the ceiling is so damaged. It's sprinkling a bit already. The piano isn't too far from the hole in the plaster. I'd die if water ruined the baby grand."

"That would be a veritable disaster," said Jane. "Go have a look, Dave." Anne tucked her arm through Dave's and headed toward the building.

Jane drove slowly down Main Street. Crooked Run was feeling more like home. She hoped the congregation wouldn't think tonight's accident had come as a divine retribution from God for hiring a female minister. She'd never doubted her calling to the ministry. When she partnered with Rick, they made the perfect team. Some days, she still couldn't fathom his absence—lost forever while attempting to rescue a young boy from a fierce current.

As she drove by the Fairchild house, she saw a strange car parked along the curb. She was almost certain Vada had said their sister Emily would arrive on Friday. They must have another visitor. The ladies sure kept themselves busy.

The lights were on in Clarence's apartment, so she rang the doorbell. There was no sound inside, so she rang once more. She'd turned to leave when she heard hesitant footsteps coming toward the front of the house. Clarence cracked the door open a sliver.

"Oh, it's you, Rev. Cartwright," he said with a sigh of relief. "I just got home." He had changed from his dress shirt and bowtie into casual sweatpants and slippers, but his face still looked tense, and a bulky, makeshift bandage covered the scratch on his forehead.

"I stopped by to see how you're doing. You had quite a scare this evening."

"Oh, par for the course in this job," said Clarence, implying that directing the choir in a small church was equivalent to engaging in frontline combat. "Won't you come in?"

"No, it's late, and I need to head home. I wanted to make sure you're okay. I guess the old ceiling couldn't handle the speaker's weight."

"Indeed." Clarence wrinkled his brow. "Our congregation should tear down and rebuild the entire sanctuary. Nay, the entire building." He looked upward as though gazing at the stained church ceiling and the old-fashioned light fixtures. "Those boards are worm-eaten, the carpets full of mold, and the foundation can barely support our meager congregation."

"The church needs to be updated," agreed Jane. "Building materials are so expensive these days, though. I'm not sure how we'd raise the money. I hope the insurance company will pay up."

"God works in mysterious ways." Clarence narrowed his eyes and gave her a sly grin.

"That he does," agreed Jane. "Now, if you're sure you're okay, I'll head back to the house."

"Yes, Rev. Go home and get some rest. You never know when Bernard might keel over and leave you to handle all the church duties."

"We all trust that won't happen for a long time."

***

"But we didn't expect you until Friday, Emily!" Vada stood at the parlor door and stared at the elderly woman on the front porch. "And who is this?" she asked as she gazed at the tall, elegant man behind her sister. He wore a gray, pin-striped suit, white shirt, and teal bow tie.

"This is Jasper Reaves, my chauffeur. I hope you have cleared out a room for him. He's driven the car for me these past two years, and I don't expect to lose him now."

"A man? In our house? Emily, you didn't mention you planned to bring a visitor. Is he.. is he your gentleman friend?" The man stepped into the light. He was younger than Emily–a dark-eyed, handsome man — maybe sixty or sixty-five. His square jaw and rather long nose gave him an aristocratic appearance. Emily's arm was tucked through his.

"Jasper is not a mere visitor! And, of course, he's not my gentleman friend! I've already told you. He is my chauffeur. He will stay with us."

Vada gasped. "Emily! We need to discuss this!"

"No, sister dear. We have nothing to discuss. There are two facts you don't seem to grasp. Number one, I am here a day and a half early; number two, I have brought my chauffeur here to stay. Now, please, move over and allow us to come inside."

Vada stepped aside and let them in.

"Who is it?" called Lillie from the kitchen. "A Bible salesman? Oh, please tell him to go away. They never sell the King James Version anymore–only the modern text that reads like a newspaper. I know some people like that style, but to me, it's just not the Bible without the 'thees and thous.'"

"Lillie! Get hold of yourself! This person is not selling Bibles. It's much more serious. It's Emily and her man."

"Her what?"

"Good evening, Lillie. Nice to see you again." Emily dropped a small overnight bag on the sideboard.

Lillie stood with her mouth agape.

The chauffeur, Jasper, spoke for the first time since their grand entrance. "I am so sorry, ladies. Emily assured me you ran a successful bed-and-breakfast and that you would have plenty of room for me to rent a space. I see that's not the case. Allow me to unload Miss Emily's belongings, and then I'll find another place to stay."

Lillie's face took on an expression of pure bliss. "Oh, listen to that accent! British to the core!"

"Why, yes, ma'am. I am from Oxford."

"Oxford, England?" gasped Lillie.

"Yes, ma'am. The City of Dreaming Spires."

"Did you hear that, Vada? Dreaming Spires!"

Vada took a deep breath, and some color returned to her cheeks. "Emily, you know we haven't operated the boarding house since Father died twenty years ago. The rooms must be filled with cobwebs and dust."

"I'll find a hotel, as I mentioned, ma'am. Later, I can check out rental properties in the area. Now, if you will show me to Miss Emily's room, I will deposit this luggage and be out of your way."

"You will do no such thing," said Emily. "We will all pitch in and clean out a suitable room for you, Jasper. It's only half past nine."

"But Emily," Vada protested, "we need to go to bed at 10:00, our usual time. We can't mix up our schedule tonight with the traumatic evening we've had. That speaker almost crushed us!"

"Then we'll have to clean fast." Emily wasn't interested in hearing the details of the falling speaker or her sisters' dramatic escape. "Now, show me to my room. I will change into work clothes, and we can start cleaning."

Lillie took Jasper's arm and led him down the hall. "You're aware she's a murderess, aren't you?"

"Who, ma'am?"

"Emily! She gave the vicar poison tea or something, right? She said

21

that's why she had to leave England and come live with us."

Jasper stifled a grin. "She told you that?"

"Why, yes! Emily said the Queen kicked her out of England because she murdered somebody."

"I'm sure it's how she saw it," said Jasper, "but that's not exactly how the story goes." He set Emily's suitcases on the old oak floor. "She gave the vicar tea with honey—not knowing he had a deadly reaction to honey or that particular honey. I believe a further analysis showed that the substance was what we call 'mad honey.'"

"Mad honey? Emily is mad. Does that make her honey mad as well?"

"No, she bought it at an open-air market. The honey contained toxins which would have made most people ill."

"So she didn't murder him?" Lillie crossed her arms as if daring him to contradict her.

"No, in fact, the chap is still alive. He spent a few days in the hospital but was no worse for the wear."

Lillie shook her head. "That's not the story she told us."

"I wouldn't dream of disclaiming Miss Emily's account, but I believe you will find my story to be a tad more accurate than hers."

Lillie shook her head. "I'm not surprised. Emily always enjoyed embellishing her stories. So you drive Emily's car? Do you work for her? How did she find you?"

Jasper smiled. "I'll give you the short version for now." He continued, "I'd retired from my regular job and found I didn't have much to occupy my mind. Emily and I both happened to be at the post office at the same time, attempting to renew our driving license. The Driver and Vehicle Licensing Agency wouldn't issue Miss Emily an updated license because of her poor eyesight. She spent several minutes trying to convince them they had a faulty eye test, but they refused to re-test her. So, we worked out an alternative plan. I needed something to fill the days, and she needed someone to drive her around town."

"Where did you work before you retired?"

Jasper hesitated. "I guess you could say I worked for the public — a public servant of sorts."

Lillie gasped. "You cleaned streets and gutters for a living?"

"Not usually." His amusement grew. "I did clean streets sometimes. I worked at Scotland Yard."

"A police officer?" Lillie's voice went up a notch.

"Yes, for 35 years."

Lillie sat on the canopied bed and looked up at the man in astonishment. "A real, honest-to-goodness Scotland Yard bobby?"

"We call them inspectors these days. But yes, a similar idea."

For the first time that evening, Lillie was silent.

"You have a lovely home." Jasper gazed around the old Victorian mansion. "It must have been a wonderful place for travelers to stay."

Lillie smiled. "Ah, yes. Some interesting people passed through these doors. I miss those days so much! I wish we could open again."

Jasper smiled. "I can imagine."

"It will be nice to have a detective in the house. We should consider taking in boarders again with you here to help us weed out the unsavory ones."

A clanging sound coming from outside the room interrupted their conversation.

"Stop dawdling, Lillie," Emily called from the hallway. "I have a bucket filled with soapy water. Let's clean this place. Shall we put him in Father's room?"

In its prime, the Fairchild House became a popular destination for business executives traveling to Washington, D.C. The Fairchild sisters had acted as maids, chefs, accountants, and general business managers of their father's "hotel," as he liked to call it.

The elder Mr. Fairchild, an old autocrat who ruled his daughters with an iron hand, passed from this life on the day the government impeached Bill Clinton. "His poor heart couldn't handle the strain," Lillie told hotel visitors. "He was so appalled that something like this could happen in the good old USA he just keeled over. Luckily, he's not alive to witness the travesty and treason in the White House today."

The sisters ran the boarding house for several years after their father passed, but they rented only one room at a time. Gradually, they found other interests in town. Lillie became an artist, Vada started a quilting circle, and Emily moved to England. Although they still enjoyed having guests, they valued their free time more. After their last regular customer, they officially closed their doors to the public.

Once in a while, the sisters heard—or thought they heard—voices and laughter in the upstairs rooms, but the ghosts remained largely silent. A self-proclaimed psychic who once stayed at the house informed them that the building wasn't haunted but did mention spirits living in the woods surrounding the mansion. None of the sisters had ever seen strange lights or dark shadows in the woods. But looks are sometimes deceiving.

***

Jane was exhausted. Her journal lay beside her bed, but she didn't have the energy to pick it up. Rev. Barnard asked her to speak at a retreat in the spring, and she should start planning. She also needed to write her reflective thoughts from the past few days. Writing always helped her process her feelings. But she couldn't slow her thoughts enough to focus this evening. She turned out the light and settled into bed. Five minutes later, her cell phone buzzed. Bethel Green. She wanted nothing more than to ignore the call, but her sense of obligation prevailed.

"Hello, Bethel."

"Jane, Olive told me about the speaker incident at the church. Is everyone okay?"

Jane sighed. The Crooked Run rumor mill ensured the whole town was most likely aware of Clarence's near miss.

"We're all fine, Bethel. Thank you for checking on us."

"I wondered," continued Bethel without acknowledging Jane's statement, "if you need a place to rehearse? I'm sure our congregation would be happy to let you use our practice room on nights we're not in it."

Jane did not want to practice in Trinity's choir room. She could see their choir members now, eyes glued to the window and ears pressed to the door, giving silent criticism to everything they heard.

"Thank you, Bethel, but the decision is not up to me."

"Will you run the idea past Clarence? I understand we're rivals, but our church is always ready to extend a hand of Christian charity when needed."

Christian charity. Is that what they called it? thought Jane. She could come up with a few adjectives she felt would be more accurate.

"Thank you, Bethel."

"Another question," said Bethel. "Do you suspect somebody rigged the speaker to fall on Clarence? I mean, he's not the most popular person right now. Lillie said he's working your voices to the limit."

"That notion has never crossed my mind, Bethel. Why would you say that?"

"I'm positive that's not the case, but I wanted to be sure you and the other choir members didn't assume one of us did it."

"One of you? Do you mean a Trinity choir member?"

"Yes, we're both preparing for the same competition, you know. And sometimes your competitor is the first person to blame if an accident happens."

"We would never think anyone from Trinity caused the speaker to fall, Bethel. The music competition is all in fun."

Bethel sounded doubtful. "Well, maybe so. But I wanted to clarify things from the beginning. Trinity Choir wants to win this contest, but we'd never stoop low enough to hurt your director or anyone else in the choir."

"We'd never accuse you of such a thing, Bethel. We're convinced whoever wins the contest will win fair and square."

"That's touching, Jane. But make sure the other choir members feel the same."

"I will, Bethel. Thank you for calling."

Jane turned off the light and pulled up the covers. Despite her exhaustion from the long and dramatic day, sleep did not come easily.

Chapter 3

Rob Randall and Chip Barker opened the popular Lucky Latte Coffee Shop as the result of a wager. A few years earlier, their favorite hangout was a small arcade in the neighboring town. The place had fast wireless Internet and wide-screen television with high-definition graphics. The atmosphere, however, could have been more inviting. A worn-out couch with cracked cushions and a scratched and stained coffee table were the only furniture in the room. The air was musty, and the walls were covered with faded posters of long-forgotten video games. The two grumbled so much about the arcade's lack of ambiance that the manager finally kicked them out. He bet them a hundred dollars they couldn't do any better.

The young men debated the idea and decided nothing prevented two intelligent individuals from starting a business. They asked a Waypoint Community College finance class to conduct a market survey to determine if folks were interested in a coffee shop or a game room. The survey results showed the locals wanted a comfortable, well-stocked coffee shop. They were surprised to learn only a few wanted a game room. The young men found a small, affordable, vacant building on Main Street, and the Lucky Latte was born. Randall and Barker framed the promised $100 bill and hung it over the door.

Jane fell in love with the Latte the first week she moved to the area. The coffee was excellent, the prices were reasonable, and the scones were to die for! Unlike the arcade, the Latte exuded atmosphere. Two small plush love seats snuggled next to a large fireplace. The brick walls were covered with local artwork, and familiar board games lined the shelves.

She and Anne were meeting there today to discuss the details of the upcoming music contest. Anne had been among the first to welcome Jane when she moved to Crooked Run. Despite their significant age difference, she appreciated Anne's enthusiastic optimism. As a church pianist, Anne bore the brunt of Clarence's ill humor. However, she only laughed at his snide remarks, much to Clarence's annoyance. She often joked that she totally defended Clarence's right to be a curmudgeon.

"Waiting for someone, Rev. Cartwright?" Jane looked up. The town mayor walked toward her table.

"Marcus. Hello. And yes, Anne should be here any minute." She wasn't in the mood to talk to the mayor. She hoped he wouldn't linger.

"I won't keep you for more than a second, Jane. I wanted to tell you I have a couple of estimates on ceiling repairs and a few quotes on new speakers."

"Thanks for taking care of this, Marcus. I can't believe what happened last night. I'm still in shock."

"I hope Clarence is okay. We don't have too many days until the big contest." Marcus's phone buzzed, but he ignored it.

"I stopped by to check on him last night. He was understandably rattled, but I imagine he'll be ready to return to practice soon."

"Guess it takes more than a near-death experience to scare Clarence." Although he spoke in a light tone, Jane sensed a note of bitterness beneath the words. His phone rang again, and this time, Marcus took the call. He almost collided with Anne as he headed away from the table.

"Sorry, I'm late." Anne slid into the booth across from Jane and picked up the menu. "Dave had a few questions about the music sound balance. I'm clueless about technology, but I tried to act like I knew what I was talking about."

"No worries. You're here now. What do you say we order a tray full of sinful sweets?"

"Wise words coming from a Rev." Anne held the menu to the light. "I'll start with a whole milk latte, topped with whipped cream and laced with a drizzle of chocolate syrup."

"Excellent choice. Jane looked with envy at her slender friend. I suppose I'll settle for the sugar-free spiced chai since just reading the description of your drink added an inch to my hips. But I want to try the marmalade doughnuts — calories or no calories."

"Ah, I like the way you think, Rev. Jane. Life's too short to worry about added inches."

"Easy for you to say! But back to the subject at hand. Dave seems like a nice guy. He must have his hands full taking care of his father. By the way, what exactly happened to Mr. Harper?"

Anne sighed. "He was a farmer. Or at least he worked on a farm. I don't think they owned any of it. Anyway, he was driving the tractor back to the barn one evening at dusk. As he crested the hill, a car came down the other side. The driver was going too fast and couldn't swerve in time. He hit the tractor head-on. Mr. Harper is lucky to be alive."

"Wow. That's tragic."

Anne nodded. "And what's more tragic is that the driver was none other than our esteemed choir director."

"Clarence?" Jane raised her eyebrows in disbelief.

"The same," said Anne. She took the top off her steaming latte.

"Wow! I'm surprised Dave still sings in the choir," Jane remarked as she sipped her spicy tea. "It would be difficult not to be bitter in the circumstances. I'm getting the idea Clarence isn't the most well-liked person in town."

"You're right there, Jane. Some people believe Clarence's business transactions are less than honest, too. When he first moved here, he told folks he dealt in highly profitable, very desirable timeshares. After he sold two or three, folks found out pretty quickly they were, in reality, old, run-down places he wanted to get off his hands. Our church custodian, Pete Jones, almost went bankrupt fixing up the two he bought. He's still trying to resell them. I doubt he'll ever get his money back."

"Oh no! That's terrible. How does Clarence justify his actions? I mean, he is a churchgoer and a choir director."

"Who knows? Pete, for one, almost stopped coming to church when Clarence started directing the choir."

"And then, I get hired as assistant minister," mused Jane. "I heard he almost quit when the church voted me in. Poor guy."

Anne smiled. "He'll get used to you, Jane. What's not to love? Clarence, on the other hand, will always be on Pete's hit list."

***

Marcus winked at the Crooked Run recreation center receptionist as he walked past her desk. "Morning, Tess!"

The young woman smiled and waved. "Josh is expecting you. Go on back."

Josh Langston was younger than Marcus, but his twenty pounds of extra weight and stringy gray hair made him appear much older. He sat with his feet propped on his desk, a cigar dangling from his lips.

"No smoking in a public place, man!"

"What?" Josh feigned surprise. "No greeting? Not even a 'How are you? Josh?'"

"How are you, Josh?" Marcus moved a pile of paper from the only guest chair in the room and sat down.

"Not too bad, considering the wife left, and the cat died." Josh dropped his cigar in an ashtray on his cluttered desk. "Maybe I'll write a country song."

"You don't have a cat or a wife, so that must have taken some real wizardry."

Josh smirked. "Better off single and pet-less. Look how you turned out. Dress shirt, spit-shined shoes, slicked down hair. I feel sorry for you, buddy."

"I get by," grinned Marcus. "Hey, I'm here to ask a favor."

"Another one?" Josh frowned.

"No, not what you think," said Marcus hastily. "Not business this time." Josh grunted.

"I assume you're aware of what happened at the church the other night?" asked Marcus, moving his foot away from a suspicious-looking stain on the rug.

"Do I look like I keep up with church stuff?"

"I thought Olive made sure everybody in Crooked Run knew about the speaker at the church falling and almost crushing Clarence Jackson."

"No great loss there, man."

"Now, that's not a very Christian sentiment, friend," said Marcus.

"I call 'em like I see 'em. I'm surprised somebody hasn't done him in before now. That old church should have been condemned years ago, too. It's a public safety hazard."

Marcus looked at the cigar smoldering dangerously close to a stack of folders. "There's more than one public safety hazard in this town. But back to the subject at hand. Our choir is trying to prepare for that big singing competition in a few weeks, and we don't have a place to practice. Can I book the room where the older adults' group meets? The one with the piano?"

Josh narrowed his eyes. "You ain't going to try to convert me to church music, are you? Because if you are, I can tell you right now it won't work."

Marcus smiled. "Who said anything about conversion? All we need is a space to practice. Monday, Wednesday, and Friday evenings."

"Well, you can't tonight. Josh appeared happy to deliver a change of plans for the choir. The seniors have a music program of some kind. Some opera gal turned folk singer or something like that."

"How about Wednesday?"

"That should work. I'll have Tess put you on the calendar." Josh looked down at his phone. "I've gotta go. Got an appointment with the boss."

Marcus stood up. "Thanks, Josh. We can talk business later. I have a lot to do today as well."

"Make sure you lock up after practice," said Josh. "Don't want any of your hoodlums messing up the place."

"My hoodlums? They're church choir members, for heaven's sake!"

Josh narrowed his eyes. "That's not what I mean, and you know it." He stood up and pointed to the door.

***

Jasper had an afternoon to himself for the first time since his whirlwind trip across the ocean. Pete's wife, Martha Jones, had invited the sisters to a quilt exhibit in Waypoint.

Jasper knew someday soon he'd have to stop and consider the cost of the move he'd so casually made. Traveling to a different country on the whim of an elderly lady went against every facet of his nature. His friends were so worried they tried to create an intervention to keep him in England. What they said was true. If Caroline hadn't moved to Scotland to "find herself," as she put it, he'd still be back at the family home in the Cotswolds.

He didn't know what had gone wrong between him and Caroline. They'd been married for twenty-five years, and he had no reason to believe they wouldn't spend the rest of their lives together. That is until she became involved with the Church of the Secret Truth. At first, she went to meetings on Sundays and Wednesdays. After about a month, she began "intensive training"--four-hour-long sessions five days a week.

Two years ago, she told him the "call" told her to move to Scotland. He later found out the "call" came from the Head Truth Imparter, who convinced Caroline she needed to follow him to Orkney's mainland. And she left—just like that.

And here he sat—four thousand miles from home, playing chauffeur to a demanding trio of aging women. He still had trouble believing he'd actually made this madcap move.

***

Jane stopped her car in front of a small, neat bungalow at the end of Main Street. Pete and Martha Jones were on her loosely constructed visitation list this afternoon. She was not looking forward to calling on the Jones family. Still, she couldn't avoid them forever. Pete was a custodian at the Crooked Run Fellowship, and Martha ran all the social committees.

Martha, a short, plump woman with tightly curled, snowy white hair, greeted her at the door. She held a poodle whose hair fell in the same pale ringlets as Marthas. "Come on in. Pete's out in the shop, but he should be in soon."

Jane patted the little dog's head, and he snarled. "Better not touch Oodles until he gets used to you. He's pretty protective. Come on in and sit

30

down."

Jane followed Martha into a tiny, cluttered living room. A large, red velvet sofa took up most of one wall, and several armchairs sat in the corners. Someone in the family collected figurines. Small resin dogs and cats filled shadow boxes on the wall. Mock plants were stuffed on a tiny wooden shelf by the window. They leaned out as though clamoring to soak sunlight into their plastic leaves.

"Well, what do you think of our town?" asked Martha. Small talk was not her strong suit.

"I love it here! The mountains are beautiful, and the people are so kind."

"Yes. No place like the Shenandoah Valley. I guess we're getting used to having you here. At first, we thought you'd be preaching every Sunday. Me and Pete don't go for women preachers. You might as well know that from the start."

"I don't do a lot of public speaking. When I co-pastored with my late husband, Rick, he handled the sermons, and I took care of counseling, planning retreats, and directing the children's choir."

Martha nodded her approval. "Sounds reasonable. We're old-fashioned here. We believe everybody has their place."

The back door rattled, and Pete Jones came in, stomping his boots on the rug.

"You take those muddy shoes off before you come into the living room, Pete Jones."

"Woman, I've been married to you for over fifty years. Have I ever walked on your carpet with muddy boots?"

Martha snorted. "There's always a first time."

Pete came into the living room in his stocking feet. He nodded to Jane and sat in the armchair farthest away from the women.

"Rev. Cartwright was just telling me that she didn't preach much. Said she took care of other church duties."

Pete grunted. "Fair enough. I think your first job should be getting rid of that sniveling, lying, cheating choir director."

Jane wasn't sure how to respond to such venom. "I heard you had a bad experience with Clarence Jackson."

Pete stood up, walked over to the fireplace, and spat into the fire. "Bad experience is only scratching the surface. That man sold me two pieces of trash property. Two houses that looked pretty good on the outside but had rotting foundations. Took all of my savings to buy them, but he assured me they would be an excellent return on my investment."

Martha had left the room and returned with a tray filled with three bottles. "Coke?" She handed Jane a warm soda. Jane smiled her thanks.

Warm sodas were not her favorite drink, but when in Rome…

"Tell her about that investment return, Pete," said Martha bitterly.

"The back deck on the biggest one caved in the first week I bought it. Had to borrow money to prop it up." Pete shook his head. "Before that shyster came to town, we were debt-free. Had been for years. Now, we owe the First National Bank of Crooked Run almost a half million dollars."

"That's terrible. I am so sorry, Mr. Jones." Jane didn't know what to say.

Pete shook his head slowly. "All I can say is that man had better watch his back."

***

"This had better be good," mumbled Marcus as he glanced around the crowded recreation center. "Practicing three times a week drains me. And now Clarence is making us come in for an extra session. You'd think we're performing for royalty."

"We picked up a bushel of late apples at the orchard yesterday. Vada wanted to try her new applesauce recipe after dinner," said Emily. "I hope they last until tomorrow."

"City girl," snorted Lillie. "We store apples in the cellar for the entire winter! Twelve hours won't make a shred of difference." She cleared her throat and stepped closer to Edith. "Remember, dear," she whispered to her fellow alto, "keep your voice soft until you're sure you've landed on the right note."

"You make sure you sing it loud enough for me to hear," huffed Edith.

Since there were no choir risers, everyone found a spot around the piano. Anne began to play warm-up scales, but Clarence was still nowhere to be seen.

Marcus paced up and down the room, pulling out his phone every few seconds. "I'll give him exactly five more minutes, and then I'm out of here. Some of us have a life."

"What is life without music?" came a voice from the foyer. Clarence strolled into the room, smiling at the group gathered to rehearse. And he was not alone. A slim, auburn-haired woman in a fashionable gray pencil skirt stood beside him.

"Good evening! Good evening!" Clarence boomed. "What a wonderful time to raise our voices in song!"

"What's gotten into him?" murmured Vada.

"I want to take a moment to introduce you to our lovely guest, Ms. Carina Vincent, professor of music at the Da Vinci Conservatory. She is here tonight to listen to you sing and to offer constructive feedback." Clarence beamed like a proud parent.

A murmur of greetings rippled through the choir, and Ms. Vincent nodded to the group.

"Butter wouldn't melt in her mouth," said Lillie, a bit too loud.

Clarence frowned. "Now, a few scales and then go straight into our warm up song, When Morning Gilds the Skies. Sing with passion! Listen to the lyrics and awaken your hearts to feel the emotion! Anne, the introduction, please!"

Despite a rocky start on the practice piece, the choir sang Ave Maria without stopping. Even Clarence looked satisfied as they finished the last measure. He bowed slightly, raised his chin, and turned toward Carina Vincent. "Well, professor, what did you think?"

She signed. "Well, that was quite the performance, wasn't it? Ave Maria is a beautiful piece, but I suppose beauty is in the ear of the beholder."

Clarence looked puzzled. "What do you mean, madam?"

"Well, first, thank you for attempting it. Although I must say, it disheartens me when a masterpiece is reduced to... well, let's call it a 'unique interpretation.'"

Clarence's face went white. "But Ms. Vincent, I believe we did a passable job. In what areas could we improve?"

Carina shook her head and sighed. "Oh, where to begin? The dynamics were all over the place. I wasn't aware that pianissimo translates to 'sing as quietly as possible.' And intonation? Well, it's a fascinating concept, isn't it? Apparently, we're experimenting with microtonality now."

"What the heck is she talking about?" whispered Edith.

"I told you she was a cold fish," said Lillie.

"We'll address these matters, of course." Clarence's voice sounded strained. "Do you have any other feedback?"

Carina tapped her red lacquered nails on the metal folding chair beside her. "Let's not even get started on phrasing. I suppose the idea of singing together is outdated. Each to their own rhythm, right?"

Clarence's face held a mixture of disbelief and dismay as Carina's words sank in. His eyes narrowed with a flicker of confusion. "Well, you have given us some things to consider," he said. "And with guidance, I have confidence we can turn this piece around."

"Guidance," she muttered. "More like a miracle from on high. Now, I will leave if you have finished serenading me for the evening. I'm late for a dinner date."

***

Clarence wasn't sure how he made it through the rest of the evening. The Harmony Choir didn't claim to be a professional singing group. Carina Vincent knew that, too. He could not comprehend what spawn of Satan entered her mind and prodded her to destroy his choir's confidence. He had anticipated condescension, superiority, and even patronage from someone like Vincent. But the venom she spat out was unforgivable. He'd hoped to boost the singers' confidence, not destroy it.

But surprisingly, Carina Vincent's disparaging remarks didn't seem to bother the choir. He wasn't sure, but he thought Lillie flashed an impolite finger at Professor Vincent as she left the room. And timid, quiet little Jen gave the woman a mock curtsey as soon as she turned her back. He'd never understand country folk—no reverence for their superiors.

The rest of the evening's rehearsal moved ahead awkwardly, to say the least. After Professor Vincent left, the singing fell flat on the very first note. Voices cracked, pitches wavered, and harmonies clashed in a cacophony of dissonance.

Clarence stopped the choir abruptly after the second page of music. "What on earth was that?" he yelled. "Are you even listening to each other?"

Jane stepped forward. "I think we've all had enough singing for now. Let's go home and rest our voices. I'm sure we'll be in a better frame of mind next practice."

The others murmured their agreement, and Clarence dismissed the group, sensing that any more singing this evening would be detrimental to everybody's mental health.

***

A cold rain lashed against the window as Clarence switched on the TV and settled to watch his favorite secret indulgence–westerns. No one would ever guess their redoubtable choir director relaxed with John Wayne. He liked the predictability and comfort of the shows. The settings never varied; the heroes stood tall, swarthy, and clean-cut. And despite living miles from any modern conveniences, the women were strong and beautiful. Villains, of course, existed, but they always received their just reward.

Just reward. Clarence's mind drifted back to the note he found on his step earlier that week. "Prepare to meet thy God." He had an idea who placed the letter on his doorstep and disliked the scenario unfolding in his mind.

Why did they bother with stealth? He was on to them. Only one of two people could have left the envelope at his front door. And if the guilty person believed their childish threats would deter him, they were mistaken. He'd come too far to turn back.

That speaker incident at church unsettled him, though. He had to believe the whole thing was a coincidence, for his own sanity. The church building was old, and a new roof had been on the agenda at every business meeting he'd attended since he moved to Crooked Run. "Not enough money in the budget," the church elders said. Maybe now they'd change their tune.

He stared at the screen as the rustlers on the TV crept up to the home-steader's cabin. Weren't they aware God was on the side of the settlers? The bad guys might pilfer and plunder in the short term, but their sins would find them out. Certain Crooked Run community members should take this to heart.

It surprised him when his phone rang at 10:00 pm. Who would call at such an hour?

A brief conversation resulted in a quick decision. If only he had given more consideration to his answer, things might have played out differently. Perhaps. But it remains an untold tale as it never came to be. Clarence grabbed a jacket and his keys and headed out the door.

The town streets were quiet. The rain had stopped, and the moon had come out from behind a cloud. Clarence rarely ventured out at this hour. Main Street looked different after dark.

Worry still plagued his mind. He'd tried his best not to keep rehashing Carina Vincent's comments about the choir. John Wayne helped, but now, away from his comfortable living room, her scathing comments rolled through his mind like a video loop. He couldn't believe she threw out words such as microtonality and pianissimo. Earlier in the evening, she'd hinted that she might ask him to be a guest lecturer in one of her advanced voice classes. He hoped she would. Payback would be sweet.

He slowed to avoid a wide oil patch in the church parking lot. Now that the rain had stopped, the full moon glinted on the pavement, causing the asphalt surface to sparkle like miniature crystals—the entire spectrum of the rainbow. Oil and water were a beautiful, though unlikely, combination. He pondered over other improbable combinations and once more questioned the late-night call.

He checked the temperature gauge on his dashboard. 32 degrees. He switched off the engine. This rendezvous had better be worth his while. Conducting a nocturnal chat on a mild summer night was one thing. To meet in the later days of autumn was another story altogether. He shivered as he walked to the door. Still, be it far from him to refuse a call for a listening ear. And who could tell what savory tidbits he might pick up along the way?

His key stuck in the lock, and his hands trembled, numb with cold. He didn't want the church alarm to go off and summon the entire Crooked Run police force — all two of them. He sighed with relief as the mechanism clicked into place.

The sanctuary was dark and damp. Shadowy, empty churches always smelled of funeral flowers. He turned on the track lights along the wall.

Someone had swept up the bits of plaster and drywall, but the enormous speaker still lay on its side, an unwieldy object in a holy place. A slight humming sound came from the stage, but otherwise, all was quiet.

The voice sounded urgent when he took the call thirty minutes earlier. It surprised him when he realized he was alone in the church. Clarence shivered. He would have worn his wool jacket if he'd known he'd have to wait. The meager fall blazer did not cut the chill, and his thin-soled shoes and short socks did little to warm his feet.

The humming grew louder as he walked nearer to the front of the church. He grunted in disgust. That careless Harrison child left the amplifier on again. He had told the boy's mother that the kid didn't need to bring that electric guitar into the sanctuary anymore. The church fathers had not written the old anthems of the faith for a pagan instrument to defile. But the boy's father supported the music ministry with regular hefty checks. He'd be a fool to bite one of the hands that fed him.

And what was this? Water on the ground? He glanced up at the ceiling, where a steady drip of liquid dropped from a strip of broken drywall. As he neared the stage, his feet began to get wet. Cursing softly, he reached to turn off the offensive noise. The moment his hand touched the metal knob, an electric surge coursed through his body, and he fell. Bright sparks flickered around the curled form slumped on the floor. The track lights crackled and went out. And then, the air fell silent - as silent and as dark as a tomb.

Chapter 4

Red and blue emergency lights flashed in front of the Crooked Run Fellowship as Jane pulled into the church parking lot. Had somebody fallen while working on the damaged ceiling? Her mind went to the elderly Fairchild sisters. They were in charge of the altar arrangements. And they usually decorated the church before lunch. "Lose an hour in the morning, and you'll be hunting for it all day," Vada Fairchild always said.

She hoped they hadn't tried to clean up the plaster debris themselves and had gotten hurt. It would be like them to tackle the mess with a dustpan and broom.

"What's going on?" she asked Deputy Brad Harris, who was putting yellow police tape over the church's front door.

"There's been an accident," he said. "Chief Smith is inside, and he asked me to keep folks out while he assesses the scene."

"What happened? Are the Fairchild sisters okay?"

Harris raised an eyebrow and looked over her shoulder. "They seem to be."

"Good morning, Jane dear," said a cheerful voice behind her. Lillie Fairchild walked toward her with arms filled with an arrangement of autumn leaves.

"Lillie! I'm so glad you're here!" Jane hugged the older woman.

Lillie stepped back and looked at her in surprise. "We wanted to come over and see if we could salvage anything from the ruins. I told Vada we shouldn't have used Mother's antique Imari vase, but if it's not broken, I'd like to fill it with leaves for fall."

"The leaves are beautiful, but I don't think they'll let you inside the building. Deputy Harris sealed off the door." Jane motioned toward the front of the church.

"Lillie, what's going on?" Vada was getting out of a sleek, black sedan. Jane was surprised to see the same car that had been parked at the Fairchild house earlier in the week.

"Something's happened at the church. Tell Emily we can't decorate today. I know that will disappoint her, but we can't do anything about it," Lillie called over her shoulder.

"Emily?" asked Jane. "I thought she wasn't coming until this evening." She glanced toward the sidewalk. The eldest Fairchild sister emerged from the front seat. A tall, distinguished-looking man helped her to the sidewalk. Jane blinked and adjusted her glasses. Who was he? She pushed her unruly curls behind her ears.

At that moment, Chief Smith appeared on the top step of the entrance-way. "Folks, I'm going to ask you to please leave the scene. You cannot access the church today."

"But we just got here," protested Vada. "We have new altar decorations. What is happening?"

"There's been an accident in the church." The chief looked grim.

"You don't mean the other speaker fell! When will the properties committee decide to fix the roof?"

"Not another speaker." Smith stepped back as rescue workers struggled to maneuver a bulky stretcher.

"Oh, no!" Jane gasped as the men moved closer. The form on the gurney was covered in a white sheet from head to toe.

"Please step back, ladies," shouted a stocky man in a paramedic uniform.

Lillie Fairchild, however, did the opposite. She moved as fast as she could while carrying an armful of silk decorations and pulled back the sheet. "It's Clarence!" she screamed. "Clarence Jackson is dead!"

"Dead?" asked Vada as though in a daze. "Clarence? But he can't be. That speaker didn't hit him. He walked away from it all."

"The speaker didn't injure him," said Harris. "I'm sure Chief Smith will give a full report soon, but right now, I can't say any more."

The women stared at each other in disbelief. Emily swayed toward the car, and the tall man rushed to steady her.

"I don't know what to think." Jane bowed her head as the red lights of the ambulance swirled in a rhythmic pattern. "Like you said, he seemed fine last night. Are any of you aware of whether Clarence has relatives nearby? I should visit them once Chief Smith has given them the sad news."

"I don't know of any relatives, although Olive Thomas told me once that she'd heard he'd gotten married." Vada looked at Lillie for confirmation.

Lillie shook her head. "He came to town alone and never mentioned a family. I doubt his parents are still living. I lost track of them when they moved away from Crooked Run 55 or 60 years ago. I'm sure the police will look into it, though."

"Well, what should we do now?" asked Vada, turning back toward the car.

"I think we should go to the Latte and have scones and coffee," said Jane. "We've all had a shock."

"You're right, Jane. I'm so distressed over what happened to Clarence. I didn't like the man, but I would never wish him dead."

Jane's eyes wandered toward the stranger who stood by Emily.

Vada started. "Where are my manners? Let me introduce you to Emily's chauffeur, Jasper Reaves. Jasper, meet Jane Cartwright, our new assistant minister."

"How do you do?" Jasper made sure Emily had hold of the car door handle before he reached for Jane's hand.

"Jasper will stay in the homestead with us." Emily smiled as though she were the cat who got the cream. "As Vada said, he's my chauffeur."

"So pleased to meet you, Jasper."

"He's British," said Emily as if Jane hadn't picked up on the accent. "Retired Scotland Yard."

"Now, that's impressive." Jane smiled. "I hope you'll enjoy staying in our little town. Did you live in London?"

"I had a flat on Victoria Street, but when I retired, I settled in the suburbs of Oxford."

Lillie broke in. "I need to inform Chief Smith we have Scotland Yard in town. I'm sure he will be most grateful for Jasper's help solving this murder."

"Murder?" chimed Vada and Jane in unison. "Whatever made you say that?" asked Vada.

"Why would they put yellow caution tape over the door if it wasn't murder?" Lillie looked indignant that anyone would dare question her verdict. "I've seen enough detective shows to know that yellow tape means murder."

"Let's hope not," said Jane. "Shall we try to forget about untimely death for a bit and enjoy a giant mug of coffee? I'll meet you at the Latte."

As she turned to leave, Jane noticed the church custodian, Pete Jones, standing in the shadow of the doorway.

***

Jane found a table near the back of the cafe and motioned for the others to follow. She appreciated the opportunity to become more acquainted with the Fairchild sisters. Vada and Lillie were key figures in the church community, and their approval would go a long way toward the rest of the congregation accepting her.

"I can't believe it. Clarence dead. What will we do about the choir competition?" Vada asked as she took off her jacket and draped it across the empty chair.

"Vada! How can you consider the competition when poor Clarence has so recently passed from this life?" Lillie looked ready to cry.

"Only a practical response, Lillie dear. I believe Clarence would have wanted us to carry on. He was so proud of the progress we were making."

"Was he now? I bet that harpy woman he had at practice last night convinced him we were a hopeless lot. And," she lowered her voice to a whisper, "I wouldn't be surprised if she didn't murder him!"

"Lillie!" Vada held a finger to her lips to silence her sister. "Don't go spreading rumors. For all we know, she might have had a headache. Maybe, in reality, she's a nice person."

Lillie huffed. "Do you believe they're rumors? You just wait until the police prove me right!"

"Ladies," said Jane, "we don't have enough information to speculate about what happened. Here comes Emily and Jasper now. Lillie, would you mind shifting over to the next chair? It might be easier for Emily to sit at the end."

Jasper helped the eldest Fairchild sister into her seat and then, with a slight bow, announced he would leave the ladies to enjoy their drinks. "There's a hardware store across the street. I'd like to check out a few garden-ing supplies. Call me, Miss Emily, when you're ready for me to collect you."

"He's such a godsend." Emily picked up a small menu lying on the blue gingham tablecloth. "Now, how am I supposed to read this print?" she grumbled as she held the paper to the light and adjusted her bifocals.

"Should I ask for a large print version?" Lillie said.

Emily frowned at her sister.

"How did you meet Jasper?" Jane asked, trying to change the subject.

"It's another story for another day." Emily glanced sideways at Vada and Lillie. "Let's say he rescued me from an unpleasant situation."

Lillie shook her head. "Not what I heard, Emily."

"Don't even start, Lillie Ruth. And what do you know? You weren't there."

"The truth will out, sister."

"And so it has." Emily half turned her chair, so her back faced her sibling. "Now, Jane, tell me about this Clarence fellow. He must have come to town after I moved overseas. I don't remember him at all."

Jane willed her eyes not to follow the tall, dapper man walking across the street and into the hardware store. "Let's see. Clarence came to Crooked

40

Run a few months before I did, so he has been here for less than a year. From what I understand, he came to Crooked Run from somewhere in the northwest. Maybe Washington State or Oregon?"

"He integrated himself quickly then," said Emily. "I like that. I like a man with a purpose."

"See where it got him?" Vada motioned for a server to take their orders.

"I can't imagine what happened," said Jane. "He was in fine form last night at choir practice. He seemed a bit disgruntled after his music professor friend said disparaging things about our singing, but he didn't give the impression he was that upset."

"I still think that music professor was evil enough to mow him down." Lillie raised her chin as if she dared anyone to contradict her.

"Mow him down? Lillie, where on earth do you get such phrasing? Are you watching gangster movies again after I go to bed?" Vada shook her head.

"My TV habits are none of your concern, sister,"

The server returned with a plate piled high with raspberry scones, and the crossfire between the Fairchild sisters paused.

"Ah, heaven in a pastry!" sighed Vada as she buttered the largest scone.

"I don't see any reason to assume someone murdered him," insisted Jane. "He could have had a heart attack. Or maybe he fell. A lot of things could have caused his death."

"Not a chance," insisted Lillie. "Why were the police on the scene if it was a health issue?"

"Law officers are required to be at any unattended death." Emily crossed her hands in her lap and looked smug.

"You would know," retorted Lillie.

"Ladies, please," Jane held up her hand. "Can we try to discuss this without squabbling?"

Emily drew in a deep breath. "I'll stop if she stops."

Lillie nodded.

"I'll be interested in what Chief Smith has to say at his press conference," said Jane.

"I doubt he'll say much. Law officers like to keep the juicy stuff to themselves. A power thing." Vada shook her head. "I think if they'd give out all the information from the start, the public could help them solve their cases in a more timely manner."

"Sometimes they're afraid too much information might impede the investigation. Assuming, of course, there was a murder." Jane sipped her coffee. The brew tasted strong, but she surmised the extra caffeine might be helpful today.

"Jane, will you direct the choir?" Lillie asked. "You're the only other person who can read music well enough." Lillie had demolished her scone and eyed the last one in the basket.

"Where did that come from?" asked Jane, her eyes widening. "Me? Take charge of the choir? I'm not qualified." She tried to ignore Lillie's hand, closing around the final pastry.

"You can read music, plus you're the assistant pastor," said Lillie, as if those qualities were the perfect definition of a choir director.

Jane shook her head. "I don't think so. I don't mind singing, but I'm not a choir leader. Besides, I'm just starting my new position at church. Surely, either Marcus or Anne will take over the choir."

"We need Anne at the piano. And if that blustering windbag Marcus leads, I will be the first in a long line of people out the door!" Vada wiped the crumbs from the table and looked sadly at the empty plate.

Lillie giggled. "Do you remember when Marcus was about three or four, and his father insisted he play Joseph in the Nativity scene? It was hilarious. Mary was 14, and Joseph was four!"

"I remember," said Vada. "He picked his nose the entire time!"

"That could explain their move to California," Lillie suggested. "His father may have thought they should be near Hollywood to increase the chance a talent scout would discover his son."

She was glad the ladies were relaxed and joking after such a troublesome morning. She glanced at her phone. 10:15 a.m.. They might have more information by lunchtime.

   ***

A bell chimed as Jasper entered the Crooked Run Hardware store. The girl behind the counter looked up. Immediately, she reached up to smooth her hair. Jasper had that effect on a lot of women. "What can we help you with today?"

Jasper smiled. "Just looking around. Passing the time." He closed his eyes and inhaled. The scent of potting soil, rubber boots, and citronella candles filled the air. Nothing could compare to a hardware store for making him remember Cotswold summers. Although the Yard demanded long hours from him, he dedicated every minute of his leisure time to his garden. He longed to feel the grainy, wet soil in his fingers again.

A loud laugh jarred him out of his reverie and drew his attention to a small group of men who sat around a metal patio table. One of the men motioned him over.

"Saw you at the Fairchild house when I passed by this morning. You visiting?"

"You might say that. I'm currently employed by Miss Emily."

42

The man leaned back in his chair and studied Jasper. "You work for 'em? You have a lot more nerve than most people in this town. Reg Reynalds is the name." He extended his hand.

"Pleasure to meet you, Reg. I'm Jasper Reaves. We're doing okay so far." He had no interest in discussing the Fairchild sisters with complete strangers.

"Better you than me," another man piped up. His badge said he was called Trent and that he worked for the Crooked Run Hardware Store.

"Say," Reg leaned in closer, "what's the latest word on that business at the church this morning? Olive said somebody got carried out on a stretcher."

Jasper nodded. "Yes, there was an incident at the church earlier today."

"And?" Reg raised an eyebrow.

"And that's all the information I have," said Jasper firmly.

"Wonder if another speaker fell?" Trent gazed upward as if he expected one of the metal joists in the store to come crashing down.

"That old church is going to cave in on itself one of these days," Reg said. "Especially since they hired that woman preacher." He shook his head in disgust. "Not to mention that choir director from hell."

"Now, Reg," said Trent. "You know the congregation voted for her fair and square. I will agree with you about Clarence Jackson, though. That man ought to be run out of town."

"Don't get me started," grunted Reg.

Trent nodded at the older man and rose to his feet. "I'd better get back to work. I have a couple of keys to cut, and they're delivering a load of feed this afternoon. Nice to meet you, Mr. Reaves."

"Nice to meet you as well." Jasper started to walk away, but Reg called out after him. "You better take care, staying at that Fairchild house. Olive Thomas, down at the post office, said one of those women killed a man. A priest or somebody. Over in England. Never trust a woman. That's what I always say."

"And we all know that you're always right." His companion slapped him on the shoulder. "I'm with you, though, Reg, on that choir director. Clarence Jackson has been trouble with a capital 'T' since the day he came to town. He thinks he's better than the rest of us since he attended a fancy music school. It's not good to give yourself airs. At least not here in Crooked Run. He'd better watch his back."

Jasper wondered how Reg and his buddy would react when they discovered what really happened at the church.

***

Jane put a load of laundry in the washer and tidied up the sitting room.

43

The afternoon was moving ahead fast. She'd just sat down for a well-deserved break when her doorbell rang. Sara's son, Brayden, stood on the front step.

"No school today, Brayden?" She opened the door wider to let the boy inside.

"Teacher workday." His eyes landed on her overflowing bookshelves. "Wow, you have a whole library in here!"

"Yes," sighed Jane. "Books are one thing I can't control. They follow me wherever I live."

"Well, I was going to ask if you would let me borrow the key to the church library. I need a copy of The Lord of the Rings. It's one of the choices for my honors English class."

Jane smiled. "I have the key. But if you want a closer option, I'm sure we can find it on one of my shelves."

Once upon a time, Jane organized her books by author name. But that was before her cross-country move. Now, her collection grew faster than she could manage it. "It has to be here somewhere, Brayden. Why don't you pour a glass of lemonade while I dig through this mess? It's on the counter by the sink."

"Thank you, Rev. Cartwright. Mom's working all day, so I decided to start the book early."

"Now that's a grand idea." Jane smiled. "I bet not too many of your classmates are that conscientious."

"Nah, most of them have a life."

"You have your music and your band, Brayden."

"We don't have a place to practice since the church is off-limits. My house is too small, and Mom doesn't ever have time to drive me anywhere else. Why can't we use the basement room at the church?"

Brayden hadn't heard about Clarence's death yet, and she didn't want to be the one to tell him. "They want to make sure the place is safe before they open it up to the public again."

Brayden didn't look convinced. "Ryan saw a light in our practice room the other night. He was afraid we had forgotten and left the lamp on. But I remember turning it off. I'm pretty careful about those kinds of things."

"I bet you are, Brayden."

"Anyway, I guess I'll go home now and start reading. I hope there's something good on TV tonight."

He turned to go and then came back into the room. "Actually, I didn't come just for the book." He looked down at his feet, not meeting her gaze. "I need to talk to you about something. You won't tell mom, right?"

"Brayden, why don't you sit in the den? It's more comfortable." She hesitated to make such an open-ended promise to the boy.

Brayden followed her down the hallway and into a cozy, plant-filled room. "Here, try out my new recliner. It has an adjustable headrest, back support, and foot lift. It has heated seats, too!"

Brayden sat down. "Man, this is nice."

"Now, Brayden, I want you to be comfortable talking to me about anything that bothers you. I will keep our conversation confidential unless it's something your mom needs to be aware of."

Brayden cleared his throat. "It's about my mom."

Jane nodded. "I see."

"I think she's having an affair with the mayor," he blurted. He gripped the armrest and continued. "She has worked late every evening for the past three weeks. When I asked her why she stayed so late, she mumbled something about learning new software. Rev. Cartwright, my mom is smart. It would never take her three weeks to learn software.".

"Those accounting programs can be complicated."

"But there's more. Mom and Marcus were at the Latte. They had their heads together, whispering. When they realized I was there, they moved apart and started to talk about Friday's football game."

Jane sat back in her chair and watched Brayden struggle with his emotions. She wanted to convince him that his mother's relationship with Marcus was purely social. But the truth was, she wasn't sure that was the case.

***

Jasper Reaves pulled out of the Fairchild driveway, careful to stay on the correct side of the road. Driving in the United States came easier than he'd expected. He'd taken a few wrong turns, but the glare of headlights approaching him reminded him to stay in his lane.

Although he had never met the man, the sudden death of Clarence Jackson intrigued him. The officers wanted to keep people away from the scene. That made sense. But was there more to it? Was foul play involved? His detective instincts were on high alert.

Jasper was glad he had the morning to explore. On his first venture, he hadn't gotten past the hardware store. Today, Emily was busy helping her sisters plan the church Christmas bazaar and encouraged him to have another look around town.

As he passed the Crooked Run Town Office and Police Department, he saw a cruiser pull into the parking lot. On impulse, Jasper slowed down and turned in behind the Chief. He should introduce himself properly. Perhaps he could find out some details about the morning's events.

Even though Chief Orie Smith was in his middle forties, he looked older. The weight of his responsibilities showed in his yellow-gray hair and stooped posture. Although his work put him in the middle of town life, he didn't have close friends. He did his job and then returned home to his double wide at the edge of town. He never married, although there were rumors he'd had a girlfriend once. One that left him standing at the altar. But nobody mentioned it now. Soon after he moved to Crooked Run, some well-meaning folks tried to hook him up with various single women. His lack of interest soon made them give up their matchmaking.

"Good morning, Chief," said Jasper, extending his hand. "Jasper Reaves. I've recently moved to the area and am exploring a little today. I work for Miss Emily Fairchild."

Chief Smith nodded and looked at Jasper with curiosity. "Work for Emily? Is she back already? I thought she was coming this weekend." Smith seemed affronted that something had happened in his jurisdiction without his knowledge.

"We're a bit ahead of schedule. Flight times changed, and we got an earlier start. I'm her chauffeur," said Jasper.

Chief Smith nodded. "Welcome to Crooked Run. I guess you didn't get a very good impression of our town if you were at church this morning. Trust me, dead bodies are not the norm. Every year, there are a couple of traffic violations, a lost cat or two, and a few domestic run-ins. Not much more than that."

"Not to worry. I've spent a lot of time coping with unexpected tragedy." Jasper wasn't sure how much to tell Smith. He didn't want to come across as pushy or a know-it-all.

Chief Smith looked puzzled. "Oh yeah? Are you a priest or a minister?"

"I've played both roles." Jasper looked down at the pavement. "I'm Retired Scotland Yard."

Smith whistled. "I should say you have experience, then. But like I said, unexpected death is a rare event in our little town."

"That's comforting." Jasper moved over to make room for a red Lexus pulling in beside the sedan.

"There's the mayor," said Smith. "The town offices are in this building, too."

Marcus got out of the car and walked toward the two men. He wore a light blue button-up shirt and gray chinos—the epitome of business casual style.

"Good morning." Smith nodded to the mayor. "Another busy day? You've been running in and out of here a lot the past few days. Guess you've got a lot on your plate with the town manager out of the country."

"Yeah, he left me a huge list. Errands to run, places to go, people to

46

see." He eyed Jasper with curiosity.

"Marcus, meet our newest community member, Jasper Reaves. He's here from England."

"Fancy," said Marcus. "Good to meet you. Welcome to the US of A!"

"Retired Scotland Yard, too," Smith added.

"Even fancier." Marcus shifted his leather briefcase from one hand to the other. "Sorry to rush, but I have to talk to some construction companies about bids on the church repairs. Fixing the roof and ceiling has moved up a few notches on the to-do list."

Smith nodded.

"I also checked with Norm Lester last night, and he says the cleaning crew will clear the debris from the church tomorrow. The insurance company has already done an estimate."

Jasper looked at Chief Smith. Wasn't Marcus aware of Clarence's death?

Smith cleared his throat. "So Marcus, I guess you haven't heard the latest news about Clarence Jackson?"

"Latest news?" Marcus looked puzzled. "What's the old buzzard done now?"

"I'm sorry to say that Pete Jones discovered Clarence in the church this morning. Dead."

"Clarence? Dead?" Marcus' eyes widened. "What on earth happened?"

Smith looked from Jasper to Marcus as though deliberating. Finally, he nodded to himself and cleared his throat. "Clarence didn't die of natural causes. I'm afraid an electrical shock did him in."

Marcus gasped. "What do you mean? Were some wires exposed when that speaker fell?"

Smith hesitated. "I don't think so. Although the fact the floor was soaked from the crack in the roof didn't help matters any."

"A hole in the roof?" Marcus looked puzzled. "The ceiling had a few cracks. Was the roof ripped, too?"

"I don't have all the details yet, but yes, the roof sustained some damage."

"Oh no! The water didn't mess up the baby grand, did it?" Marcus looked concerned.

"No, it missed the piano. It puddled in front of the stage, though." Smith hesitated, then continued, "I plan to make a statement at a press conference at noon today, but I will tell you now. They found Clarence with his hand on a frayed wire that connected to an amplifier plugged into a live socket."

Marcus stared at the chief in stunned silence.

"But wouldn't the breaker trip and kill the power before it completes the circuit?" asked Jasper.

"The church has ancient wiring. It still has a fuse box. The Fire Marshal warned us it was only a matter of time until the entire system blew." Marcus shook his head. "He gave us a break because it's a church. Any other organization he'd have written up long ago."

"I'm not an electrician, but shouldn't the fuse have blown before the shock became fatal?" asked Jasper.

"In the right circumstances, it would have. But we discovered something strange in the electrical panel. We found a penny behind the fuse, which completed the circuit. It appears someone disabled the fuse on purpose." Chief Smith looked from one man to another as if trying to gauge their response to this news.

"Do you mean murder, Chief?" Jasper stared at Smith. "Do you believe someone set up the system so it would electrocute Clarence?"

"I'm afraid that's what it looks like," said Smith. "It's early days, though. We still have a lot to investigate."

"That's awful!" Marcus's paled. "I know he frustrated some choir members. He has pushed us pretty hard these last few days. But nobody was that angry. Who would want to hurt Clarence?"

"That's the million-dollar question." Smith tugged at his collar as though he wanted to loosen the top button. "One we will need to answer as soon as possible."

"I don't know what to say." Marcus seemed rooted to the ground, all thoughts of his busy day behind him.

"Like I said, we still have a lot of gaps to fill. Anything I say now is pure speculation. Please keep this information confidential," said Smith. "The folks at the Crooked Run Chronicle will hound us soon for information, but I want to hold them off as long as possible. We have to look into the situation more closely before we can conclude someone murdered Clarence."

"Wait a minute." Marcus tapped his forehead as though a new idea had entered his mind. What about that homeless man folks have been seeing around town? Anybody check him out?"

"We will question anybody we need to," said Chief Smith. "Just don't start any rumors until we have the facts."

"I know this is presumptuous," said Jasper, "but if I can do anything…?".

Smith nodded. "Appreciate the offer, but we'll likely call in the State Police if we don't come up with any leads by tonight. As I said earlier, we're not used to violent crime in Crooked Run,"

Jasper nodded. "Fair enough. Best of luck, sir, in your investigation. Thank you for welcoming me to the community. I'd better head home, or

Miss Emily will assume I'm neglecting my duties."

"A pleasure." Marcus shook Jasper's hand as he turned to go. Jasper glanced at the two men in his rear-view mirror as he merged onto the highway. Unlike the American justice system, Jasper considered everyone guilty until proven innocent.

As he passed the church, his eye caught what appeared to be a bundle of clothes piled against a street sign. Parking beside the heap, he saw the jumble of clothing was actually a figure wrapped in flannel and denim. Most likely the stranger Marcus mentioned. The man raised a hand in greeting, and Reaves waved back. He'd have to ask the ladies about that. Who was this person? And why was he here in Crooked Run?

***

The evening sun sank behind the Blue Ridge Mountains as the choir members gathered at the Fairchild house to discuss their next steps in the choir competition. Everyone appeared curious about what would happen, and the large room was already filling.

"Jasper, bring another chair from the back room. We're running out of seating." Vada hurried into the parlor, balancing a tray of small sandwiches in one hand and a teapot in the other.

"So someone killed him. I was right," said Lillie smugly.

"The Chief didn't come right out and say murder."

"He didn't say he died of natural causes, either."

"I'm sure Chief Smith will reveal more details as he can." Jane took the teapot from Vada and set it on a small end table.

"So, what are we going to do? Keep singing or give it up?" asked Vada.

"Give up the choir or the competition?" Edith asked as she poured a minty liquid into a delicate teacup.

"Either? Both?" Vada removed Charcoal the cat from a wooden rocker and sat beside her friend.

"What would Clarence want us to do?" asked Anne. "We all know he was a passionate musician. This contest meant everything to him."

"So I take it you're voting to continue with the competition?" Deputy Brad Harris took a small cucumber sandwich from a silver tray and leaned back in his chair.

"I haven't made up my mind yet," said Anne. "But I'm convinced that Clarence would have wanted us to continue."

"We've already mastered the hard parts," said Edith. "Now, it's a matter of practicing it until it's perfect."

"Perfect is a bit of a stretch," said Vada. "But we're making progress. It would be a shame if we canceled it now."

"We have this overarching problem, though. We don't have a leader."

Anne rose and walked toward the window, peering at the darkening sky.

"Jane should lead us," said Lillie. "That's what I've been saying all along. She's musical, and she doesn't yell. Besides, Rev. Barnard hasn't seen fit to share the pulpit yet."

Jane blushed. She hoped they wouldn't get into a discussion about women in the ministry. Assuming that she could lead the Harmony choir was bad enough.

"Now, that's the most brilliant idea I've come across all day," said Brad. "You've led choirs before, haven't you, Jane? And you've been at every practice."

"My choir-leading experience was a long time ago." Jane shifted in her seat. "And with a children's group. I haven't directed for years. There's a big difference between singing in a choir and leading it."

"But you're so talented," said Lillie. "Even Clarence said you were the only choir member with a sense of timing. That was a big compliment coming from him."

"We'd be great followers," Jen smiled. "As Edith said, we've already learned the hard parts."

"What about Marcus?" said Jane. "He likes to take charge. By the way, where is he?"

"He said he had to drop off some books at the library," said Sarah. "He'd checked out a few on electricity and soundboards. He's trying to help Dave figure out what new equipment we'd need to get our sound system up to speed."

Young Brayden Floyd looked uncomfortable. "I don't want to be rude, but Mr. Marcus needs more than library books. He didn't know the difference between an aux knob and a fader."

"A who from a what?" asked Lillie.

"Oh, it's tech stuff." Brayden's face turned red. "They're parts of a soundboard."

Jane wondered if Brayden had come to the gathering to make sure his mother wasn't meeting up with Marcus after work hours.

"But back to the subject at hand," said Anne. "I'm sure Marcus would be glad to have you lead us. He is so busy with town operations, especially since the manager is on vacation. What do you say, Jane?"

The parlor door opened, and Jasper entered the room with the eldest Fairchild sister on his arm. "Greetings, all," said Emily. "Sorry, we're late. Everything takes longer these days than it did twenty years ago." Jasper helped Emily to a wing-backed chair and handed her a cup of tea. "Now," she continued, "don't worry, I have this choir dilemma all sorted out for you. I have a few suggestions to make it all turn out for the best."

"Emily," scolded Lillie, "you're completely ignorant about this situation! You just got here on Wednesday evening."

"You doubt me, dear sister? I was always the one to fix Father's accounting issues. Why, I saved the boarding house from ruin many times."

"It's a long step from accounting to music, sister," snapped Lillie.

"I'm not saying that I'm a musician, Lillie." Emily narrowed her eyes. "I have always had a logical mind and can sort out tangled webs. Here's our winning plan for the choir's first-place trophy."

"First prize is much more than a trophy, Miss Emily," said Brad, filling his plate again. "It's a European trip to several of the great cathedrals."

Emily closed her eyes. "Ah yes, Notre Dame in Paris, St. Stephens in Vienna…" Her face took on a dreamy expression. "That's almost enough to make me join the choir."

"What's your idea, Emily?" asked Vada. "We're all on pins and needles."

"No cause for sarcasm, sister. Now, listen. You all agree that Jane should lead the choir; I'm not saying you're mistaken. But she should lead it with the help of another excellent musician, Mr. Jasper Reaves." She paused as if she expected a drum roll. All eyes turned to the chauffeur.

Jasper looked down at the floor. "You've got it all wrong, Miss Emily. I've had no experience leading a choir. I love music, but it's all just a hobby."

"Your voice is magnificent, Jasper. I heard you singing Moon River yesterday while you were sorting the spring bulbs in the garden shed. You have the voice of an angel. Jane can direct the timing, and you can lead the music. What do you say, Jane?"

Jane glanced over at Jasper. He still looked uncomfortable, tapping his foot against the fireplace ledge. She could feel her cheeks turning red. What was this sudden return to teenage awkwardness? She cleared her throat. "Do you read music, Mr. Reaves?"

"Call me Jasper, please. And yes, I can read music."

Jane sighed. "I'm not qualified to lead a choir. Not even close. However, I'll try it, but only for the competition. I am not making promises about the future. Is that understood? My first commitment will always be to Rev. Barnard and helping shepherd the Crooked Run Fellowship."

"Of course, Jane," said Vada. "One step at a time. What about you, Jasper?"

Jasper looked at Jane, who nodded. "If the lady believes I can assist, I will gladly help. But please, don't set your expectations too high."

"Good," said Emily. "It's all settled. The music goes on."

"I hope we're doing the right thing." Jane looked doubtful. "I guess we can continue to use the rec center until the church is available again?"

"I believe that's what Marcus told us," said Brad. "But I'll double-check with him on Monday."

"It's too late to work on anything tonight. If you're free, we can meet at the church in the morning to review the music, Mr. Reeves. I assume they will let us go into the choir room? Is 10:00 okay?" Jane looked at Jasper.

"Wonderful! Just don't expect too much. I'm rusty and out of practice."

After everyone cleaned up the refreshments and said their goodbyes, Jane drove the two miles back to her house in thoughtful silence. She should have been listening to her practice tape, but her mind was full. Accepting the job as choir director was a decision that usually would have taken weeks of pondering. But she didn't have weeks. Not even days. The competition was looming, and the choir needed a director.

***

"It was nice having everyone over this evening." Lillie stretched out in her recliner and sighed with contentment. "Hearing laughter in these rooms brought joy to my heart. Vada, I miss having people in the house. Do you suppose we could ever open the boarding house again?"

"I don't know, Lillie. We have Father's trust to cover our expenses, but we're not getting any younger."

"I suppose we have the option to hire someone to do the hard work. The money has accrued interest for over two decades. Jasper might have some ideas."

"Possibly," said Vada. "We need a miracle or a sign. Do you think it's possible that Emily bringing Jasper here is a start?"

"Having a man around the house would make things easier. Let's consider our options and meet with Emily and Jasper. Maybe we can come up with something. We've lived alone for many years, though. I don't know if I'm up to having people around all the time."

"Do you remember the guests we used to have?" Vada's eyes took on a faraway look. "That family that came back every summer? Those two kids were so spoiled. They said we were primitive because we didn't have a color television set."

"But those were fun times. Father never meant for us to close the boarding house. That's why he left that money."

"It's a big step, Lillie. Especially at our age."

"But we have a good support system with Emily and Jasper here. Please consider it, Vada." Lillie's voice held a pleading tone.

***

Anne sat in her car and watched a few remaining autumn leaves land on her windshield. She glanced at her phone. Still no message from Dave. They'd planned to meet at the Fairchild house and then go to dinner. She liked Dave, and she thought he liked her as well. What went wrong? She sighed. Well, there's no point wasting a beautiful night. She'd drive into Waypoint and have dinner. Alone.

***

The ex-Mrs. Clarence Jackson looked around the cheap motel room. She reached the Virginia border but still had a long way to go to Crooked Run.

Poor old Clarence. When the officer appeared on her doorstep, she was sure he was coming about the jury duty she'd failed to attend. Her mind had raced through possible excuses. Migraine? The car wouldn't start? Sick aunt? She hadn't thought of Clarence in ages.

The young man seemed nervous. Perhaps this was the first time he had ever delivered news of a murder. A murder? Someone had murdered Clarence? She still hadn't wrapped her head around that.

She also hadn't processed the call she'd received from Clarence's attorney earlier that day. Clarence had left her money! A lot of money. Where had that come from? And why her? Why didn't he leave it to his beloved Julliard? Clarence always prided himself on being a starving artist during the brief time they'd been married. He must have changed his outlook. Had it not been for the money, she wondered if she would have attended his funeral. She wasn't greedy. All she wanted was what she deserved.

Gloria Jackson folded a fuchsia pink sweater and returned it to her overnight bag. She'd save that for the memorial service. Clarence had always hated pink. But he'd hated a lot of things. Rock music, dry white wine, toy poodles — everything she loved. Maybe that was why their marriage had ended soon after it started. Still, she felt she owed him a last goodbye.

She threw the suitcase in the back of her Tesla and started toward the highway—the road to Crooked Run.

Chapter 5

Anne's house was dark when Dave pulled into the driveway. He hadn't expected her to wait up for him—he was three hours late for their date. And he'd missed the gathering at the Fairchild sisters' house.

He turned off the engine and sat in silence. The air chilled after the sun went down, and he shivered. Part of him was glad he had a few hours to contemplate how he would explain his absence to Anne. Telling her the truth was not an option. As those thoughts crossed his mind, he realized for the hundredth time he was in over his head.

His eye caught a faint flicker in an upstairs window. Perhaps she was awake after all. His phone buzzed. It was Anne.

"Are you coming in?" her voice was taut.

"Do you want me to? It's after midnight."

"What do you think? You're three hours late. I deserve some explanation."

And therein lies the issue. He had no explanation to offer. Not a true one, anyway. "Sure, I'll come on in."

Anne still wore jeans and a white cotton blouse. He felt a twinge of remorse when he realized she had waited up for him.

"Are you hungry?" She sat a plate of cookies on the coffee table.

He took a bite of the still-warm cookie, but his guilt caused it to feel like sawdust in his mouth.

"I guess the obvious question is 'Where were you?'" said Anne. "So I'll start there."

Dave wanted to come clean and explain to Anne where he was and what he was doing. But he couldn't—she would never understand. "Dad got worse," he said finally. "I had to sit with him longer than I'd planned." The minute he said the words, Dave wished he could pull him back. Why had he lied? He half expected lightning to streak through the window and strike him down. He deserved it.

Anne's expression changed to concern. "Oh no, Dave. I'm so sorry! What happened? You should have called. I'd have joined you."

"I'm sure you would have." Dave lowered his head. "I never expected I would be that long, but Dad kept feeling worse. He would have insisted I go if I told him we had a date. I should have called you, but didn't want him to overhear and feel guilty about keeping me from our dinner."

"You must be exhausted," said Anne quietly. "Go home and get some rest. I'll stop by and check on your dad tomorrow."

Dave nodded. "Please don't mention our date. He thinks he's tying me down, anyway. It will make him feel worse."

Anne watched Dave's headlights as he backed out of the driveway. His story was plausible. His dad was not making any progress. She would have bought the entire tale if she'd not seen Dave's car on the way to Waypoint last night. The car was parked at Denny's Digs — a cheap hotel outside the town limits.

***

The morning dawned sunny. Jane took her coffee to the back deck and stretched out on a lounge chair overlooking a woodland stretch. She enjoyed the wildlife that visited her bird feeders, especially the squirrels. At first, she had tried to discourage the hungry little rodents, but the more she observed their antics, the more she appreciated their company. Now, they darted up and down the poles, stuffing their cheeks full of birdseed. She closed her eyes and her thoughts turned once more to last night's gathering at the Fairchild house.

What made her agree to lead the choir competition? The group's trust in her musical abilities brought her joy, but was she prepared? Clarence coached them through the challenging parts of the song, making her job more manageable. But still....

And what about Jasper Reaves? Jane wasn't entirely sure how he fit into the picture. Miss Emily had them all under a spell. Everything she said made sense in the dim, cozy parlor at the Fairchild house. Now, in the light of day, she wasn't so sure. He said he was able to read music, but could he sing? Suddenly, Emily's plan seemed a little unstable. Jasper was an attractive addition to the Harmony choir, but his dimpled chin and crystal blue eyes wouldn't win the competition without some musical talent to back them up.

She sighed and took her coffee mug back inside. She'd have to leave soon to meet Jasper at the church. This morning, a call to Chief Smith cleared the way for them to enter the choir room. He was adamant that they avoid the sanctuary and make their meeting quick.

Jane drove slowly down the road. Crooked Run was beautiful in the fall. Red maples, blazing in shades of crimson, gold, and orange, lined the streets. The Lucky Latte's storefront glowed with reminders of the season. Pumpkins of various sizes and colors lined the front steps, and hay bales wrapped with strands of twinkling lights lit up the walkway.

When Jane arrived at the church, two state police cars were parked near the entrance. The Fairchild's black sedan was also there. At least Jasper was prompt.

"Greetings," called Jasper as he got out of his car. "Lovely morning!"

"Indeed." Jane said as she fumbled in her purse for the church's back door key.

"Pardon me if I don't know quite what I'm doing in this venture," Jasper smiled. "When Miss Emily says go, I go, without always knowing why."

"She is one commanding presence." Jane smiled. "My goal for the morning is to find Clarence's copy of the anthem and to go through his notes. Perhaps you can help me decipher his directions for the choir."

The music room was dark and chilly, contrasting with the weather outside. Jane and Jasper had no trouble finding Clarence's choir binder and notebook. He clearly did not expect anyone to review his notes. Jane cringed at his comments: 'Edith sounds like a wounded animal on the second measure of page two,' 'Sara needs to wipe the frown off her face–fake joy if she needs to.' 'Lillie drones on after the last measure–remind her to cut it off sharply.'

"This Clarence sure had some strong opinions," said Jasper, looking over Jane's shoulder. Jane caught the scent of sandalwood soap. She forced herself to turn her mind back to the music. "Yes, I shudder to consider what he made of my singing. I wish we could skip past the personal jibes and only see his musical notations."

"I hope he didn't actually say those things to the choir members," said Jasper. "He sounds as critical as his professor friend."

Jane grimaced. "Clarence had few filters. Still, I don't think he would have been that blunt."

As Jane turned the last page of the binder, a piece of paper fluttered to the floor. "Well, what have we here?" she said as she bent to pick it up.

The note, which appeared torn from a composition book, had cut-out magazine letters with the message: "Prepare to Meet Thy God."

***

Dave Harper had cleaned up the lunch dishes and settled his father in front of a gardening show on TV when his phone buzzed. The ID screen showed the words Crooked Run Police Department. He froze. He wanted to ignore the call but knew it was no use.

"Hello, Dave here." He walked into the back bedroom, out of his father's earshot.

"Dave. This is Chief Smith. We need you to come down to the police station right away."

"Uh, OK. Can you give me a hint of what this is about?"

"We'll talk when you arrive. I expect you within a half-hour."

Dave walked back into the living room. "Dad, would you be okay if I stepped out for a bit? Work called. They need me to troubleshoot a problem."

Mr. Harper smiled at his son. "What would they do without you, Dave? Keep on, and you'll be mayor one day."

Dave gave his father a half-hearted smile. "No danger of that, Dad. I won't be long."

When Dave arrived at the police station, Chief Smith was waiting for him. "Come back into my office, Dave."

"What's this all about, Chief?"

"Sit down, Dave, and we'll talk." He pointed to a chair in the corner. Smith stared at Dave for a long minute and then pulled something from his desk drawer.

"Does this belong to you?" He held up a small wrench enclosed in a plastic bag.

Dave nodded. "Yeah, that's mine."

Smith looked closely at Dave. "Are you sure? Take your time."

"No, it's mine. It has a splotch of green paint at the bottom of the handle. That's how I mark my tools. Where did you find it?"

Chief Smith didn't answer at first. He continued to search Dave's face. "Were you aware it was missing?"

"I don't do a tool check every night, Chief. I don't use that wrench set often. It might have been missing a long time before I realized it was gone."

"Did you use this at Crooked Run Fellowship anytime from Wednesday morning until Friday morning?"

"No, I fixed a short in Clarence—uh, Mr. Jackson's—amp, but the tools I needed were much smaller than that wrench. Where did you find it?" repeated Dave.

"We found it beside the hot-wired amp on the stage."

"What? A hot-wired amp? Do you mean...are you saying that Clarence touched a hot wire? That he was electrocuted? That's awful! What happened?"

Chief Smith narrowed his eyes. "I was hoping you could tell me."

Dave stood to his feet. "What? Me? How would I have any information about that? I haven't been inside the church since Wednesday evening."

"Did you lend your wrench to anyone?"

"No, it's not even a very good wrench. It's one of those cheap department store tools. I'd be ashamed to let somebody borrow it."

"Dave, can you account for your whereabouts during the past few days?"

"Wait. Are you accusing me of having something to do with Clarence's death?" Dave crossed his arms and glared at the Chief.

"I'd like for you to write a statement telling us in some detail where you were and what you have done since Wednesday evening."

"This is ridiculous," said Dave.

"Mr. Harper, this is not a request. It's an order."
***

Jasper and Jane sat at a small round table in the back of the Lucky Latte, the torn composition page in front of them.

"We need to take this to Chief Smith. It's likely evidence he'll need," said Jasper. "But I want to take a quick photo of the paper before we turn it in. Smith was adamant that he did not want or need any help from me in solving this crime, but I can't help but wonder if an outsider's perspective might be helpful."

"Something to do in your spare time?" Jane sipped her cherry almond latte.

"Miss Emily makes sure I have precious little spare time during the daylight hours," he chuckled. "By the way, it shows how much she admires you, allowing me to spend the morning with you working on music."

"Is she aware that we're also having coffee?"

"I fear there is little Emily Fairchild doesn't know." Jasper smiled.

"Jasper, do you think someone from Crooked Run killed Clarence? Word on the street is that he was murdered."

Jasper poured sugar into his black coffee and stirred. "Police still need to gather a lot of information before they can determine for sure what happened," he said carefully. "Although it may appear to be a straightforward case on the surface, I will need much more evidence before I come to any conclusions."

"Spoken like a true detective," said Jane. "By the way, were you a detective or an inspector? The British police hierarchy is confusing."

"Detective Chief Superintendent."

"That sounds impressive. Is it?" she grinned.

"Some may have that perception. But it's only a title." He glanced out the window and then looked back at Jane. "Can you come up with anyone who wanted Clarence out of the picture? Did he have any enemies?"

"I don't know if Clarence had enemies, but many folks found him irritating for various reasons. Still, most people don't go around murdering individuals that provoke them."

"Some people get triggered by surprising things," Jasper snapped a picture of the plastic-covered note.

The lunch crowd had not yet entered the cafe, and Jane was glad she wouldn't have to explain her tet-e-tet with Jasper to curious minds. Crooked Run was a classic small town in every way. One simple glance at her and Jasper together would be enough to set the rumor mills running. She didn't need any more complications in her life right now.

"I'll drop the note off at the Police Department on the way home." Jasper put the plastic bag in his pocket. "I should be going. I'm sure Miss Emily will call me soon."

"Someday, you'll have to tell me more about how you and Miss Emily connected. I'll bet it's a fascinating story," said Jane.

"Depends on how well I tell it," he smiled.

As they stood to go, Jane realized they hadn't picked up the choir robes from the church. "Wonder if they'll let us back in the choir room to get the robes? We haven't used them in months. They probably smell like moth-balls. I'll need to have them dry-cleaned."

"I'll ask when I drop this note off. And Jane," he hesitated, "Thanks for trusting me to help with this choir adventure. I know I'm a complete stranger to you, but I promise to do my best to keep the music moving along."

"I'm glad you're part of the group, Jasper. It might take two of us to handle the job, but we'll be fine."

Jane glimpsed the strange man across the street again as she walked to her car. This time, he appeared to be watching her specifically. Despite the daylight and despite being in a public place, she shivered.

***

"Why didn't you give this to me sooner?" asked Chief Smith as Jasper handed over the note he and Jane had found in Clarence's choir binder.

"We just discovered it this morning," said Jasper. "In the choir room."

Smith grunted. "My team searched the whole place. Where did you find this?"

"Someone tucked it in the director's notebook, among the music notations and individual singer observations."

"And that's all you know about it?"

"That's it. We looked through the entire director's book and found nothing else."

"Why didn't you bring the book?" asked Smith. "That might be evidence as well."

"There's nothing in it but the music score and Mr. Jackson's notes."

"That's for us to decide. Now, Mr. Reaves, I know you retired from Scotland Yard. But you have no jurisdiction here in the United States. I appreciate your willingness to help, but you can't withhold potential evidence."

"Of course, sir," said Jasper.

"Now, as soon as Harris comes back in, I will send him over to collect the notebook and any other relevant evidence we might find. Please stay out of the church until my office gives you the go-ahead. Is that understood?"

"Yes, sir. Can you ask Deputy Harris to put the choir robes out where we can pick them up? We will need to have them cleaned for the choir competition, and we forgot to grab them this morning."

"We'll be sure that the choir gets their robes. Now, goodbye, Mr. Reaves."

"Good day, Chief Smith."

As Jasper drove back to the Fairchild house, he wondered at the downright unfriendliness of the Crooked Run police chief. Did a retired Scotland Yard detective threaten him?

He should let Jane know the police planned to take the notebook. He was sure she'd want to make copies of Clarence's notes. The late director was a tyrant, but many of his musical notations made sense. He checked his watch. He had time to make the copies himself.

***

Dave sat on a picnic bench under a sprawling maple tree in the park. His eyes took in new graffiti scribbled on the bridge supports. "Crazee Byrds," A music group? A gang? He didn't remember anybody in his high school class ever spray painting bridges. But times had changed.

His visit with Chief Smith had rattled him. From the law's point of view, he looked guilty. There was no way around the fact he'd been messing with the amp. The same amp that fried Clarence. The wrench puzzled him. He hadn't used that set in a long time. Who could have taken it from his toolbox and put it on the stage? Was somebody trying to incriminate him in Clarence's death? He pulled his jacket closer. An icy wind came from the northwest, reminding him that winter was closing in on Crooked Run.

"Can't sit out here too long in this fall breeze, Dave. You'll catch a chill."

Dave looked up to see Mayor Marcus Justice on the path in front of him. He had been so lost in his thoughts he hadn't noticed the older man's approach.

"Got a minute to talk business?" Marcus sat down on the opposite end of the bench. Marcus, as always, wore an impeccable outfit. Dave looked ill at ease in his torn jeans and flannel shirt.

"Yeah, I guess," Dave mumbled.

"Hey, we can meet another day if this isn't a good time to talk."

"It's as good a time as any. What's up?"

"I was wondering how much it will cost to replace the speaker. The one that fell the other night." Marcus took out a small notebook and glanced at a column of numbers.

"Are we talking about replacing the speaker or the whole electrical system? It's all outdated."

"I'd like to replace every piece of the system, but I'm not sure where the money will come from." Marcus kicked over a rock as if searching for the errant cash.

"The properties committee says our number one priority is to replace the roof and the ceiling," Dave said. "There's been a lot of water damage. We can't put the speaker back up until the structure is stable."

"I've got Sara working on a grant to help pay for the roof. The church will have to do some fundraising, too. We got a little money from the insurance settlement, but not enough to replace everything."

"I'll find prices on speakers and systems and get back to you. I doubt the choir will sing in that space for a while."

Marcus said, "Speaking of choir, I've reserved Mondays, Wednesdays, and Fridays for practice at the rec center for the next two weeks. It differs from Clarence's schedule, but those were the only evenings the rooms were free. Are you going to make it over Monday night? I might have a more solid budget by then."

Dave lowered his head. "I'm thinking about dropping out."

"Of the choir?"

Dave nodded.

"What do you mean? We need all the male voices we can get. I understand it must have been awful finding Clarence's body and all, but the choir needs you."

"That British guy who lives with the Fairchild sisters is going to sing. They say he has a powerful bass voice. They don't need me. Besides, it's hard to leave dad these days. His condition is getting worse."

"I'm sorry. That must be tough. But nobody knows for sure if that Brit can even sing. Those Fairchild sisters don't always see things like you and I do."

"Thanks. I'll think about it."

"And one more thing, Dave. What's this about Chief Smith finding your wrench near the spot where Clarence died? What was it doing there?"

Dave's eyes widened. "He told you already?"

"We share an office space, Dave. Look, I'm not accusing you of anything. I simply want to find out what is going on in our town."

Dave shook his head. "I have no idea. I didn't put it there. I don't use those cheap tools anymore. Somebody is trying to frame me."

"Who might that be?" Marcus looked at the young man. "And why would someone try to frame you?"

Dave stared back. "I have no clue. Do you?"

Marcus shook his head. "You need to be careful who you hang out with, Dave."

***

Brayden wished he had some idea of what was bothering his mom. For several months, he'd thought something was going on between her and Marcus. But now he wasn't so sure. He'd seen them together at the office; sometimes, his mom looked like she couldn't stand the mayor. When he leaned over her shoulder to look at a spreadsheet or a grant proposal, she'd shrink away like the man was poison or something.

Brayden knew she was trying her best to shelter him from her worries. Ever since his dad left, she tried to keep life steady and predictable. But his dad did nothing to support the family. Why should he? He'd already started a new life. Brayden and his mom were old news.

But Brayden's instincts told him that her anxiety went beyond tiredness and lack of money. He'd catch her staring into space, an unreadable look on her face. She'd also missed his last parent-teacher conference. Most kids would be glad if their parents didn't talk to their teachers. But except for honors English, he was doing really well in school this year. He'd been kind of eager for his mom to meet his teachers.

He didn't think her preoccupation had anything to do with the upcoming choir competition either. His mom didn't let things like that bother her. She was late again this evening. He pulled some burritos out of the freezer and preheated the oven. At least he could make some dinner.

He switched on the TV as the local news cut into the afternoon cartoons. "We interrupt this program to join a press conference with the Crooked Run Police Department. They have updated news regarding the death of local choir director Clarence Jackson. And now, here's our Police Chief, Orie Smith."

"Good afternoon. On Friday morning, October 20, Pete Jones, the Crooked Run Fellowship church custodian, found choir director Clarence Boyd Jackson, 65, unconscious on the floor of the sanctuary. Paramedics determined Jackson had no vital signs, and Dr. Herbert Brewer pronounced him dead a quarter of an hour later. Preliminary investigations show Jackson died of electrocution because of a faulty wire connecting an amplifier to a power outlet. Police are continuing to investigate the incident, but the death is now considered a homicide. We will keep you updated as more information becomes available."

Whoa. Old Clarence Jackson is dead! He wasn't a fan of the choir director, but he didn't want him to die. And someone murdered him. Wow. He wished his mom would come home soon.

Chapter 6

Rev. Barnard had permission to hold services at the church on Sunday but not in the sanctuary. The congregation met in the fellowship hall amid sheets, robes, shepherd's crooks, and other Christmas pageant paraphernalia. Some members thought they should skip the service this week out of respect for Clarence, but most folks were glad for a bit of normalcy.

"Surprised you're here, Pete," said Norm Lester as he moved his long legs to the side and let the older man slide into the chair beside him. "I wasn't sure you'd be back since the vote didn't go your way."

Pete Jones snorted. "I never imagined I'd live to see the day we had a woman behind the pulpit in Crooked Creek. The founding fathers would turn over in their graves."

Norm chuckled. "Gotta move with the times, old fellow. Speaking of graves, what are your thoughts on old Clarence passing away right here on the stage?"

"I can tell you this much. I was right spooked at finding his body all sprawled out on the floor like that."

"That's right. You were the one who found him. I always believed this wiring would zap somebody before it was all said and done," said Norm.

"Didn't you hear the press conference yesterday? It wasn't an accident. Somebody rigged it so Clarence would touch the wrong wire at the wrong time."

"You mean somebody murdered him?" Norm sat upright. "How do they know?"

"Reggie told me they found a penny behind the fuse in the panel box. Completed the circuit. Electricity from the amp ran right through him."

Norm shook his head in wonder. "Well, I'll be. I knew Clarence was a cranky old thing, but I didn't think anybody disliked him that much. You'd better clean up your act, Pete. If somebody has it in for grumpy old men, you'll be next on the list."

Anne began to play the prelude. The music sounded thin and reedy on the cheap portable keyboard. A record number of people turned out for the service, whether out of curiosity or the need to be together during a tragedy, no one could say.

The music stopped, and Rev. Barnard rose to speak.

"Friends, it's with a heavy heart that I come before you today. I'm sure you will join me as we mourn the loss of our friend and choir director, Clarence Jackson. As you are aware, Mr. Jackson met an untimely death on Friday morning right here in our church. Even though Clarence was with us for less than a year, we all have grown to respect and appreciate his leadership in our music department. Just last week, I sat in the back row and listened to your lovely rendition of Ave Maria. I believe Clarence would be happy if you would continue with the competition. I understand that was a tough decision, and I applaud your courage–especially the courage of my assistant pastor, Jane Cartwright, who has graciously agreed to lead you in the competition."

The rest of the service was short. Several people spoke about Clarence and how his talent had moved the choir to a new musical level. Although most folks acknowledged Clarence's contributions, no one appeared particularly sorrowful at his passing.

On the way to the parking lot, the police chief motioned for Jasper to join him beside the cruiser.

"Will you be okay walking to the car, Miss Emily?" asked Jasper. "Chief Smith wants to talk to me."

Lillie grunted. "My sister can get around better than Vada and I put together. She fakes a limp for attention."

"Lillie Ruth, you have no idea how much I have suffered," Emily said. "I put on a brave face for the world, but I'm aching inside."

Jasper nodded to Chief Smith and then took Emily's arm. She turned to smirk at her sister.

After he settled the still-squabbling Fairchild siblings, he went to join Chief Smith again.

"You got your hands full," Smith nodded toward the car.

"Yes, you might say that," said Jasper.

"Listen, Reaves, I know I told you I didn't need any help with this case. And possibly, it will turn out better than I expected. But let's just say that it doesn't. Let's say the pieces don't fall into the puzzle. I might need to ask for

65

your advice once in a while. Is that okay?"

Jasper nodded. "Of course. I'll do whatever I can."

"I suppose you're aware we've confirmed that Clarence's death was, indeed, a murder."

"I listened to the press conference yesterday afternoon. Maybe since people know Clarence's death wasn't an accident, it will trigger some memories. People often see more than they realize."

"It will also bring the crazies out of the woodwork," Chief Smith shook his head. "I'm going to bring that homeless man in for questioning."

"I saw him the other day. Does anyone know him?" asked Jasper.

Chief Smith looked out over the parking lot. "That's what I intend to find out. As far as we can tell, Clarence had no living relatives. But keep your ears open. The Fairchild ladies know everybody and their great-grandma. Let me know if you find any information that might be helpful to the case."

"Again, Chief, I'll help in any way I can. Keep me updated."

Chief Smith nodded. "Will do. And thanks."

***

Gloria Jackson was sure nobody had recognized her at the Sunday service. Why would they? She'd never visited the small town her ex-husband had moved to. She'd slipped in during the first hymn and left before the benediction. Why had Clarence come to this remote town? They didn't even have a proper restaurant. Perhaps she'd drive back to Waypoint for a late lunch. She wondered what she'd do with her time until Clarence's funeral. Tomorrow, she'd meet with the attorney. She'd know more then.

Chapter 7

Jax didn't have a last name. At least one he used anymore. He'd shed that part of his life years ago. Shed it along with his family relationships and his old identity. He couldn't tie himself down to anything or anyone, including a job. Everybody wanted money these days. He remembered when he could barter with one of his hand-drawn caricatures or a carved wooden figure. But not anymore.

Jax perceived things. He sensed things. As a young child, he'd been able to read a room within seconds. He could tell when his dad was about to lash out at his mom before his dad even opened his mouth. His sixth sense was more of a burden than a blessing, though. People mistrusted him. They didn't like people who could peer into their souls. He didn't invade their thoughts on purpose. He just knew. And his knowing made them uncomfortable.

Jax didn't see visions. Sometimes, he wished he could; that insight would give him more confidence when people asked him to do difficult things. But the call was clear. Someone had tracked him down. That, in itself, was a miracle.

Getting across the country was a trial. Long-haul truckers refused to pick up hitchhikers, especially ones who looked like Jax, with his heavy backpack and shopping bags full of belongings. A lonely driver offered him a ride as far as Kentucky. Jax didn't love listening to country music for thousands of miles, nor did he care for the tobacco spit that collected in the small Coke bottle in the front cup holder. But the trucker didn't talk much, and Jax slept a lot on the journey.

The driver left him at an all-night truck stop, but first, he bought Jax some sausage gravy and biscuits. He also put a ten-dollar bill beside his plate—a modern samaritan.

Various short rides and too much walking got him to his destination–a little burg tucked into the hills of the Shenandoah Valley of Virgínia. Crooked Run.

The person who'd called him didn't want to meet him publicly. Didn't offer him a place to stay. So, Jax set up camp under a bridge in the park. Even though the nights were frosty, the mid-November days were still mild. He hoped he would find lodging by winter. If plans worked and promises were kept, he wouldn't have to worry about the cold again. If they didn't… well, he'd think about that if he needed to.

***

Time stood still in the law offices of Mills, Mills, Mills, Mills, and Estrada. Gloria Jackson paused in the foyer and gazed at the grand waiting room ahead. A crystal chandelier sprinkled pale light rays on a worn but expensive-looking Persian rug. Several dark bookcases held ancient-looking, leather-bound volumes. Even the dust motes that danced in the filtered sunlight looked old.

"Mr. Mills will see you now," came a voice from behind a large desk. Gloria hadn't noticed the small woman among the looming pieces of furniture. "This way, please."

She led Gloria down a long hall past a row of portraits of distin-guished-looking men. The secretary stopped before an open door and motioned for Gloria to go in.

"Hello, Mrs. Jackson. I'm Ryder Mills. We spoke on the phone earlier this week. Please sit down."

Gloria looked around the spacious room. Like the foyer, shelves of legal tomes lined the wall, their spines glowing with embossed gold lettering. A mahogany desk occupied the center space, and a vintage brass lamp cast a pool of light over a stack of legal documents.

"First, allow me to express my condolences over the loss of your hus-band."

"My ex-husband," Gloria corrected. "We hadn't seen each other for years."

"Nevertheless, he must have had some lingering feelings for you." Ryder Mills smiled.

"Not sure why," said Gloria. "But go on."

"As I told you on the phone, Mr. Jackson made significant financial arrangements before passing. He left you a substantial sum of money in his will."

Gloria took a deep breath. "Again, I must say I am shocked."

Mills nodded sympathetically. "Sometimes, people express their care and regret in unexpected ways," he explained. "It's clear Mr. Jackson wanted to provide for you, even after his passing."

Gloria wanted to tell him that their relationship wasn't like that, that the Clarence she knew wouldn't have left her a wooden nickel. But obviously, something had changed in his financial status and in his heart. Who knew what motivated men like her ex-husband?

"Everything is included in this folder," Mills said, handing her a large portfolio. There is also a sealed letter addressed to you. "Take your time with the documents. If you have any questions or need further assistance, please don't hesitate to reach out."

Gloria took the documents and stood to leave.

"Mrs. Jackson," Mills said, "there is one more thing. As you will see, you have inherited a substantial amount of money. I would advise you to make your own will in the near future."

Chapter 8

Jane spent most of her spare time working on the nuances of the choir's rendition of Ave Maria. Schubert's harmonic language in the song was rich and nuanced. Clarence had arranged the harmonies for multiple vocal parts, but the choir still struggled to balance their voices. Smooth transitions between the chords were a challenge as well.

This morning, She invited Anne over to help work on these problematic areas. Jane's old upright piano was not quite in tune, but it would be adequate. She glanced at the clock on the mantle. Anne wouldn't be here for another thirty minutes. She brewed a cup of coffee and stepped onto her back deck to enjoy the beautiful morning.

Tomorrow evening would be the first choir rehearsal without Clarence. Bethel Green called three times in the past three days with information about the contest. Each time, Jane assured her that Clarence had left detailed instructions in his director's file. Bethel was also curious about Jasper Reaves. Again, the town gossip grapevine proved effective. News of the dashing British co-director had piqued the curiosity of the competing choir.

Jasper was attractive, no question. He would be quite the hit with the female choir members. He could also read music, which was even more critical.

A loud clanging sound interrupted her reverie. She looked down to see a man standing near the deck. He wore layers of clothing—a dingy black and white flannel shirt over a black T-shirt. Around his neck was a frayed purple scarf, and he wore dirty gray sweatpants. He held a backpack with various pieces of tinware hanging from the bottom–the source of the clanging noise.

The homeless man. The man who had scrutinized her for several days. Jane knew that the sliding door was only a few feet behind her. She could slip inside and lock up before he reached her.

But something about his look stopped her. His deep brown eyes held a calm intelligence that lessened her fear. The same man that looked so menacing in the gathering dark last night looked harmless in the light of day.

"Not to startle you, ma'am. But I wondered if you'd let me rest here for a minute." Before Jane could answer, he put his backpack on the ground and sat down on the bottom step.

"Name's Jax, ma'am." He stretched his legs out and removed his shoes.

Jane felt the comfortable bulge of her cell phone in her pocket. If worse came to worst, she had the option to call 911. And Anne was due soon.

"You must be new here," said Jane.

Jax nodded. "The call came, and I obeyed. I go where I see a need."

"A need?"

"The universe calls on me to set matters straight. There'll be a void or an injustice, and I come to set things right."

"What kinds of things?" asked Jane. Talking to this strange man might not be prudent, but she was intrigued.

"It varies." Jax was agitated. He picked at the zipper on his backpack. Jane hoped he didn't have a gun or a knife in there. He hadn't elaborated on how he planned to 'set things right.'

"Where did you come from?" She asked, hoping to steer him back to a safer topic.

"Out in the western desert."

"You've traveled a long way. I'm sure you didn't walk. Do you have transportation?"

"The Lord provides," Jax said matter-of-factly, as though the Lord's provisions were a daily gift.

"Did someone from Crooked Run call you to come? If so, it looks like they would have helped you get here and arranged a place for you to stay."

"The Lord moves in mysterious ways."

Jane closed her eyes. She'd heard that phrase recently. Where?

"Did you choose to stop at my house on purpose?" asked Jane. "Why did you come to me?"

"I'm camping out in the park. I followed the path in the woods. It brought me to your place."

"Who else do you know here?" Jane tried to be polite and unthreatening, but if this stranger had the nerve to walk up to her house and make himself comfortable on her steps, she would be direct, too.

71

"Not any longer," was his reply. "But I have not yet gotten the call to leave, so I will stay here until I do."

"What do you mean?" asked Jane, puzzled.

"The man who summoned me has left the earth."

"You mean he died?"

"In God's holy house."

"Do you mean Clarence? You were friends with Clarence Jackson?"

"Friends? No," came the curt reply.

Jane heard a car pull around the front. Good. That would be Anne. She wondered if she should leave Jax on the back deck or ask him to move on. Perhaps she should invite him inside for coffee.

Someone banged on the front door. That was odd. Anne rarely knocked.

"Excuse me. I need to go let my friend in." Jax had put his shoes back on. "I won't be a minute."

Jane was surprised to see Chief Smith and Deputy Brad Harris on the porch.

"Good morning, Rev. Cartwright," said Smith. "Sorry to disturb you, but there have been reports that the homeless man might be in this area. Did you happen to see him this morning?"

"Why, yes. He's on my back porch." She motioned for the two men to follow her through the living room and out the sliding doors in the back.

The deck was empty. Jax was gone.

"Excuse me, ma'am, but there's no one there. Are you sure you saw him?"

"Completely sure. We were talking." Jane shaded her eyes from the morning sun and peered into the woods. But Jax was nowhere to be seen.

Smith looked interested. "You talked to him? About what?" he asked.

"Truthfully, I'm not sure. Jax said someone contacted him to come here, but the individual who had summoned him was not here anymore."

"Did he say where this person went?"

Jane shook her head. "In a manner of speaking. He said the person who called him here was no longer on the earth."

Chief Smith's eyes widened. "No longer on the earth? Is this person deceased? Was he talking about Jackson? Did Clarence call him here?"

"I don't know. We were getting to that part when you and Deputy Harris arrived."

"Well, he obviously didn't want to see us," said Harris. "That doesn't bode well for his innocence."

Smith nodded and wrote something in his notebook. "And what else did he tell you?"

72

"He quoted the Lord a lot. Seemed to think he had a direct communication to him."

"What did he say?"

"Something about the Lord providing and the Lord working in mysterious ways. Why are you looking for him? Is he in trouble? He said he'd set up camp under the bridge. I suppose that breaks some kind of vagrant law?"

Smith looked at Harris. "We are regarding him as a suspicious person in connection with the death of Clarence Jackson. He might be dangerous. I'd be more careful about who you allow on your property. Harris," he nodded to his deputy, "send out an APB."

Jane heard a car come up the driveway. That would be Anne.

The officers thanked Jane for the information and pulled out just as Anne's car stopped.

"Wow, Jane! What was that all about?" Anne hugged her friend and took a plate of muffins from the car.

"The police are looking for Jax, the homeless man. Mmmm! Those muffins look and smell delicious!"

"Wait a minute, Jane. You can't get off that easily. First, how do you know the guy's name, and second, what do the police want with him?"

"I am familiar with his name," said Jane, taking a bite of a buttery muffin, "because he was on my back porch only minutes ago sharing his life story with me."

Anne's eyes grew wide. "That man was at your house? He knows where you live? Oh, Jane, you can't stay here alone. You're not safe now that he's familiar with your address!"

Jane patted her friend's hand. "I appreciate your concern, Anne, but I'm perfectly safe here. He's harmless."

"If he's so harmless, why is Chief Smith trying to find him?"

"I don't know, but I talked with Jax. He seems delusional–all those voices he claims to hear–but he has a caring heart. I can tell."

"Jane, you are so unworldly. You spent too much time in seminary discussing angels on pinheads and not enough time in the real world. That man could be dangerous. Did you forget we just had a murder in our church?"

"I didn't forget, Anne. And I've been in the ministry long enough to experience the 'real world,' as you call it."

"So you don't believe he killed Clarence?" Anne put two scoops of sugar in her tea and stirred it.

"He's not the type, Anne."

"But he ran when the police came."

"True. However, Jax may have had negative experiences with law enforcement in the past. They don't have a lot of sympathy for unhoused people."

"Jane, they have to protect the town."

"I'm so sorry for Jax. He's sure that someone sent him to Crooked Run for a purpose. His 'mission,' he called it."

"But do you reckon his mission was to kill Clarence? I've come across stories of individuals who believe God is telling them they need to eliminate certain people."

"I have no clue what to think, Anne. I hope the police can soon clear things up. Now, before we start on the tough parts of Ave Maria, tell me what's happening with you lately. Are you nervous about the choir competition?"

Anne sighed. "No, it's not the choir. Do you remember I told you I've been talking to Dave, the sound guy?"

Jane nodded.

"Well, we've started to see each other more frequently."

"He seems like a pleasant fellow."

"I thought so, too. Until…"

"Until what, Anne?"

Anne sighed. "We planned to meet at the choir gathering at the Fairchild's house. Afterward, we were going to dinner at the new Mexican place in Waypoint."

"I didn't see him at the Fairchild house," said Jane.

"That's just it. Dave wasn't at the Fairchilds. And he didn't show up for our dinner date either. At least not when he was supposed to."

"Did he call you later and explain?"

"That's the strange part. He came to my house a little after midnight. Said his dad had gotten worse and that he had to stay with him."

"That's understandable, but why didn't he let you know?"

"Dave said he didn't want his dad to think he was messing up his son's social life. He didn't want him to think he was interfering."

"Why didn't he make a quick call out of his dad's earshot?"

"My thoughts exactly. But that's not the worst part." Anne put her head in her hands.

Jane patted her shoulder, encouraging her to go on.

"I was restless when Dave didn't show up at the house. I took a drive around town. I saw his car, Jane. It was parked at Denny's Digs, that cheap hotel between here and Waypoint. What is he up to? Why did he lie to me, Jane?"

Chapter 9

Dave tucked the fast-food bag under his arm and unlocked the front door. The dark, musty apartment depressed him, but his dad wouldn't allow him to open the curtains. "I don't want the neighbors to look inside and pity me," he said.

Right after the accident, Zander Harper seemed to have lost the will to live. He was paralyzed from the waist down but showed no interest in learning how to compensate with the abilities he still had. On some days, Dave had to feed him to make sure he received proper nutrition.

But now, Dave believed he could sense a slight positive change. The elder Harper still had days when he slipped back into a dark depression. He was grateful; however, those days were fewer and fewer.

"What are you feeding me for lunch today, son?" Dave sighed with relief. Today was shaping up to be a good day.

"Burgers and fries, Dad." He set the bag of fast food on the TV table. "Thought I owed you a proper meal after the burnt toast and weak coffee this morning."

"Appreciate it, son."

Dave felt pleased with his dad's eagerness to open the bag and start eating.

"Did you learn anything else about that murder down at the church? They said it was a murder, didn't they?" Zander bit into his burger.

"Yeah, I reckon so." Dave wasn't in the mood to talk about Clarence Jackson. Not with the proof of Clarence's carelessness sitting right in front of him in the wheelchair.

"Can't imagine the man had many friends, but I didn't think folks hated him enough to kill him," said Mr. Harper. "If anybody had a grudge against him, it should be me." He looked down at his useless legs.

Dave grunted, trying to come up with a way to change the subject. "Guess the church will have a new roof after all."

"I always said that the old church needed an update. Hanging that speaker on rotting wood was an accident waiting to happen. And I doubt anybody has looked at the wiring since they built it in the 30s. Something bad was bound to happen, eventually."

"Pretty sure the old wiring didn't have anything to do with Clarence's death, Dad."

"What I don't understand is how they're sure it was murder. Mr. Harper dumped his french fries onto a paper plate and poured ketchup on top. "Seems to me that an accident would be most likely with a fuse box as old as that one."

"They have their ways, Dad. Listen, I'm exhausted. Can we change the subject? How is your fantasy football team doing?"

"Haven't kept up with it much, Dave. Can't get my mind to focus on it."

"You were pretty excited when we picked the teams."

"Yeah, but that was before the accident."

"Dad, the doctor says you're doing great."

"Maybe physically. Mentally, I go down some dark holes."

"Yeah. You have way too much time on your hands. Too much time to worry. We need to check into getting a motorized wheelchair so you can get out more. Maybe you can drive again."

"You mean a van, right?" his dad said contemptuously. "These useless legs won't ever push the gas pedal on that hot little sports car down at the garage."

Dave understood that nothing he said would cause his dad to change his perspective. He wasn't surprised at the older man's quick mood swing. Those switches happened a lot since the accident. His only option was to wait until his father was in a better mood and try to talk him into looking ahead. Heaven knew they couldn't afford a vehicle his dad would be capable of driving. He would need to be patient and hope for the best. Someday, his ship would come in.

On a brighter note, Chief Smith had gotten off his case. Dave wrote a detailed account of his activities before and after Clarence's death. His story seemed to satisfy the policeman—at least for now.

***

Brayden was supposed to meet the guys at the park to practice, but the clouds were getting darker, and he could already feel a few raindrops.

He didn't want the Gibson to get wet. He'd walk back to the house. His mom wasn't due home until after five p.m. It would be closer to six if things continued as they had been the past few weeks.

"Evening."

Brayden looked up to see a man dressed in several layers of tattered clothes standing on the walking trail before him.

"Hi," Brayden said. He knew he wasn't supposed to talk to strangers. Even though he was at least six inches taller than the little man, the guy might have a gun or a knife or something.

"Music is good for the soul." The man eyed the Gibson.

"Yeah, I guess so," mumbled Brayden.

"I'm Jax," said the man. "I do the Lord's work."

"That's good, I guess." Brayden took a few steps away from him. "But it's raining. I need to get home."

"The Son of Man hath nowhere to lay his head."

"Right," said Braydon. "Well, I should be going."

"Wait," the man came closer. "I have been called here for an important mission. I thought the mission was over, but I have found more to do. Do you know any place where I might stay out of the cold?"

Brayden shook his head. He felt a little sorry for the man. "Did you check with the Town Office? They can sometimes tell you about housing and such. My mom works there."

The minute the words left his mouth, he wanted to take them back. He didn't want a tramp knowing where his mom worked.

"No help from them," came the reply, and Brayden was relieved.

"I'm not sure, but I can ask around. I'll let you know if I find anything." All he wanted to do was get away from the man. "Where do you stay now?"

"I camp out in the park." The man pointed to a heap of clothes under the bridge. He was lucky it had been a dry summer, or the river bed wouldn't have been an option. The top of the walking bridge offered him a small amount of shelter. Brayden bet if Mayor Marcus had any idea the guy was living at the park, he'd make him move. He was sure that Chief Smith would evict him as well.

Just then, Brayden saw the town police car circle near the park. Jax noticed it, too. And before Brayden could tell him goodbye, Jax was gone.

Chapter 10

The Crooked Run recreation center was abuzz. Jane already sensed that this practice would differ from the silent, tense evenings they rehearsed with Clarence.

"Oh, hi, Jane," said Jen. "This place is awesome! Look at the lighting! I won't have to squint to read my notes."

"I'm not sure why Clarence kept the lights so dim the last time we practiced here." Jane deposited her jacket and director's notebook on a folding metal chair. "Can someone find a podium or something I can use as a lectern?"

"What about this?" Deputy Brad Harris unfolded a tall music stand. "Not perfect, but it will do until we can return to the church to practice."

"Why can't we practice at the church? They let us have services in the fellowship hall on Sunday," said Lillie.

"Lillie, the fellowship hall isn't connected to the main church building," Vada said as she moved past her sister and settled into the soprano section.

"Still," said Lillie, but a loud bang from the piano cut her voice off.

"Sorry, ladies! Just warming up my fingers," said Anne, running up and down the scales. "I like the sound of the old uprights, but nothing can match my Baby Grand!"

Jane checked off the choir members—Brad, Dave, and Marcus—for the bass, baritone, and tenor sections. Altos: Edith and Lillie; Sopranos: Sara, Jen, and Vada. There were eleven participants, including Jasper, Anne, and herself. They met the competition's minimum requirement but with no one to spare. Everyone had to stay healthy!

"Were you aware," said Emily from her seat at the puzzle table in the back of the room, "that Ave Maria is not a religious piece?"

"What do you mean, Emily?" Vada stood with her hands on her hips as though ready to defend the honor of the song.

"I don't believe that's a hard concept to understand, Vada. Listen carefully. Schubert didn't write Ave Maria as a religious song."

Emily's proclamation caused a murmur of doubt among the choir members.

"Schubert wrote it about Sir Walter Scott's poem 'Lady of the Lake.' The Catholic church has a prayer with the same name, so they used the song as a worship piece."

"Leave it to you to take all the glory out of our music, Emily," said Lillie.

"Not at all." Jasper smiled. "Scott's poem has a section that includes a young girl's prayer to the Virgin Mary. That part is a worship piece."

Emily snorted. "Believe what you wish. I shall tune you all out and work on this jigsaw landscape. It will no doubt fit together better than the pieces of your music."

"Thanks for your vote of confidence." Vada glowered at her sister.

Jane knew she had to create order, or the Fairchild sisters would bicker the entire evening. "Ladies and gentlemen, we need to start our practice. We can discuss the pros and cons of the song later. Clarence chose it as the piece for the competition, and it is the piece we have practiced—regardless of religious or non-religious connotations. Now, let's sing our warm up hymn, When Morning Gilds the Skies."

Practice went better than Jane had expected. For the most part, everyone stayed on pitch. Jasper's voice was rich and intense, and his confidence made the entire men's section more robust. Sara's soprano solo was beautiful and poignant. Jane's one significant change to Clarence's arrangement was moving Sara to lead soprano. Mary's song required a sense of reverence, tenderness, and emotional intensity, and Sara's voice delivered that exact tone.

"Too bad the snippy professor missed out on this session," said Anne. "We'd have blown her socks off."

"You mean her Pradas?" Sara laughed.

"Her what's?" asked Jen

"Pradas–those $900 tights models and movie stars wear." Sara laughed at Jen's puzzled expression.

"People pay that much for tights? Why?"

"Prestige, I guess." Sara continued, "If I had $900 tights, I'd be sure to wear the tag on the outside so everybody would know how much I paid for them."

"Ostentatious." Jen looked down at her worn jeans. "I think I'll stay with my style—Crooked Run Shabby Chic."

"Should we keep up Clarence's three-night-a-week schedule since we are so close to performance time?" asked Jane. "It's strange moving ahead as though nothing has happened. But we need the practice to perform well in the competition. Is everyone okay if we add an extra practice day?"

"It's a fabulous idea," said Anne. "We still have some rough parts to smooth out."

"Wonderful. Can we meet on Friday evening, same time; same place?"

There was a murmur of agreement among the choir members.

"That was a great practice, Jane," said Jasper, staying behind to help her lock up. "We should be more than ready when the time comes to perform."

"Do you really think so? Thank you so much for your help," she said, locking the rec center's door behind them.

The night was crisp and clear. Jupiter appeared in the east, and the Big Dipper stood out on the northern horizon. A million stars peppered the sky.

"Beautiful night," said Jasper as he walked Jane to her car. "There is supposed to be a meteor shower later on."

"I always miss those," Jane said. She knew Jasper was standing close. She could again smell the scent of sandalwood.

Silence filled the space between them while they gazed at the night sky. As if on cue, Jasper's phone buzzed. "Ah, it's Miss Emily. Imagine that. Goodnight Jane. I'll see you tomorrow."

As Jane backed out of the parking lot, she caught a flash of lights in her rearview mirror. Several police vehicles lined up along the road to the Crooked Run Community Park. She wondered if they'd picked up Jax.

***

Jax had gone with Chief Smith without incident. The night was freezing, and he felt thankful to be indoors, even if it meant being at the police station. He'd asked if it would be possible to spend the night in a cell and answer questions in the morning. Although his request was unusual, Deputy Harris and Chief Smith found no reason to refuse it.

"Reminds me of the Andy Griffith show," said Harris as he settled Jax into the cell for the night.

"Unfortunately, Aunt Bea won't bring you chicken potpie, though," said Smith, as he put a frozen dinner in the microwave. "Turkey and gravy with mashed potatoes and stewed apples."

Jax ate the T.V. dinner as though the food were a gourmet meal. "Don't mean to cause trouble," said Jax between mouth fulls. "Much obliged that you let me stay the night."

Smith nodded. "Forensics results will be back in the morning. If we find any trace of your fingerprints on the crime scene, our setup won't be nearly as cozy."

"I can sleep the sleep of the innocent, Chief. I did not kill Clarence."

"Can you tell us what you are doing in Crooked Run? It's a strange time for a vacation. Winter is coming on, and you don't have a place to stay."

"I have nowhere to lay my head." Jax wiped the gravy from his mouth and eyed Chief Smith's still-full plate.

"You still hungry? I can put another one of those TV dinners in the microwave."

"That would be most wonderful," said Jax. "I haven't eaten in a while."

"Want some coffee, too? This stuff is not the best, but it'll warm you up."

Jax nodded.

Chief Smith liked this funny little man despite his better judgment. At first, he was sure the stranger was the killer. But as he watched the thin, elderly man devour a frozen turkey meal with the gusto of someone feasting on a New York strip, he doubted his theory had much substance. He handed the coffee to Jax.

"Well, at least you'll have a decent place to sleep tonight. We'll talk in the morning. I hope you're telling me the truth. If that's the case, then you're free to go. If we find a crack in your story, this VIP treatment will stop."

Jax nodded. "I told you before, I have no blood on my hands."

Smith nodded and picked up his coat. "I'll see you bright and early."

Jax sat back on the cot, pulling the thin blanket to his chin. The Lord's work was never easy. Nobody promised him a bed of roses. Like he told the Chief, he had no blood on his hands. But his hands weren't clean, either. A deep stain marred the surface. Soap and water wouldn't wash it away.

Tonight, he was safe. His stomach was full, and he had a cot, pillow, and blanket. He wouldn't ponder anymore about his stained hands tonight. He would pull the cover over his tired body, close his eyes, and sleep.

Chapter 11

"Jane, dear, what kind of tea would you like? I have Earl Grey, Lady Grey, and Lillie's mint leaves from the garden."

"Thanks, Vada. I like the sound of garden mint," said Jane as she sank into an overstuffed recliner in the parlor of the Fairchild house.

"It will be you, Lillie, and me for tea today. Jasper and Emily have gone off to town."

"I didn't expect tea, Vada. I planned to collect the choir robes and be on my way."

"Marcus said he tried to drop them off at your house, but you weren't home. It wouldn't have hurt him to have them dry-cleaned himself. His wife is out of town, but he could have handled it."

"It's fine," said Jane. "I don't mind taking care of it."

"By the way, they arrested that homeless man at the park." Vada set a tea tray filled with blueberry scones on the coffee table. "Edith called this morning. Her apartment is close to the police office, and she saw the Chief taking the man in."

"I had a short conversation with Jax the other day. I don't think he had a motive to kill Clarence."

"You talked to him?" Vada's eyes were wide. "Weren't you afraid?"

"He seemed pretty harmless to me," said Jane as she bit into a blueberry scone. "These are heavenly, Vada. Did you bake them?"

"Yes. It's an old family recipe. We used to serve them at the boarding house. Father said that some guests returned year after year just to eat the scones."

"I can sure understand why. But back to Jax. He came to my house the other day. We had a few minutes to chat, but when Chief Smith showed up looking for him, he disappeared."

"Very suspicious," said Vada.

"Maybe, but sabotaging an amplifier doesn't seem like Jax's style. Plus, nobody reported having seen him in the church."

"He pretends to be religious, though. The man doesn't do himself any favors by always quoting the Lord. Pete Jones said he was in the hardware store the other day trying to convert the store manager."

"His comments are sometimes jarring." Jane buttered another scone. "Sometimes he talks like a regular person, and sometimes he goes into a sort of prophet mode, talking about the Lord's work and how he's supposed to fulfill some mission."

"That doesn't endear him to Chief Smith," said Lillie, coming into the room carrying a dripping paintbrush.

"Lillie, take that paintbrush to the sink, for heaven's sake! You're dripping paint all over the rug!"

Lillie took the offending brush to the kitchen, calling over her shoulder. "What if his mission was to murder Clarence and rid the world of that cranky man?"

"Lillie, that's not very Christian of you. Maybe Clarence didn't have a stable home life. Not everybody had the same wonderful parents we had," Vada said.

"Father was a benevolent tyrant," said Emily. "But at least he was predictable. We never had to wonder if we'd have enough to eat or a warm house to live in."

"I have some news," said Lillie, returning to the living room. "I don't know if there's anything to this, but Olive told me today that Clarence has an ex-wife."

"Really?" said Vada with genuine curiosity. Lillie had everyone's attention now.

"Yes, and that's not all. Olive said she's in town!"

"Here? In Crooked Run?" Jane asked. "How does she know? Where is this ex staying?"

"She's at the hotel at the edge of town. Olive said she saw her go into the lawyer's office, too. Wonder if she inherited any money?"

"People don't leave money to their ex-wives, Lillie."

"They do if they're still in love with them," said Lillie stubbornly.

"Clarence did well for himself. He studied at Julliard. I'm sure that wasn't cheap." Jane poured a stream of amber liquid into her teacup.

"Maybe he got a scholarship. What if this Jax had a connection with him when he was young? What if he followed him here to kill him?" Lillie sat down on the sofa across from Jane.

"That sounds a little far-fetched, but stranger things have happened." Charcoal jumped onto Vada's lap and started his daily bath.

"So many speculations." Jane sighed. "This is lovely, ladies, but I need to head out. I'll pack up the choir robes and be on my way. I will check into the rumor about Clarence's ex-wife. If she is here, I should pay her a visit."

"The robes are in a box on the sun porch," said Vada. "If you wait until Jasper returns, he can carry them to your car for you."

"I'll be fine. Thanks for the tea, ladies!"

***

As Jane entered the Crooked Run Town office, dark clouds covered the sky. The meteorologist hinted at the possibility of early snow. So much for the mild fall weather.

She had been trying to meet with Marcus for two days. Sara finally found a spot between nine and nine-thirty, so Jane made it work. Marcus had volunteered to take care of travel plans for the choir's trip to the Virginia Beach competition. The time was getting closer, and although Jane was sure he'd work out the details, she would feel better when she could look at the schedule herself.

The town hall was one of the few modern buildings in Crooked Run. After fire destroyed the original municipal offices, the town wrote a grant for a sleek, contemporary stone and glass building. The money awarded by a Community Development Foundation matched the building cost estimate. Still, after erecting the frame, the funding fell short of the actual cost. So, while the outside of the building was polished and modern, the inside was a patchwork of cheap plywood and thin drywall.

"Jane, please have a seat," said Sara, noticing Jane standing by the door. "Marcus's meeting is wrapping up."

Despite the soft music playing in the waiting room, Raised voices came from behind the thin office door. Marcus was not having a friendly conversation with the person inside. Jane hoped his animosity wouldn't carry over to her meeting.

"How is Brayden doing in school this year?" she asked Sara, hoping to lessen the awkwardness.

"Like most kids his age, he thinks he'd rather be doing something else. But he's doing well. This year, he's part of the guitar club and enjoying it. He's big into music theory now."

"He should join our choir," said Jane.

Sara laughed. "We're way too old-fashioned for Brayden! He and Clarence had different opinions on how to play music and which instruments to use in worship."

85

"It wouldn't hurt our choir to try modern pieces sometime."

"So, are you planning to be the permanent choir director, Jane?" Sara moved a pile of papers off her desk and set another stack down.

"I'm taking it one day at a time. We need to survive the contest first. I may do such a terrible job that you'll be glad when it's all over."

"I don't believe that for one minute." Sara smiled. "You're doing an amazing job."

Marcus's office door opened, and the voices became louder. "I don't want you to come back until you have a solution to the problem, Dave," Marcus said. "There's no reason you can't move ahead as we planned."

Dave, red-faced and angry, didn't answer. He nodded to Jane as he strode past her and out the door.

Marcus shook his head. "I'm sorry for Dave. He has a lot on his mind. I'm sure caring for his dad takes a lot of energy. But when you pay a man for a job, you expect him to do it right."

Sara looked up. "What's going on?"

Marcus glared at her. "He's supposed to install a new sound system at the elementary school."

Sara raised her eyebrows. "Oh, that's news to me. I haven't filed any paperwork on that project."

"You don't know everything," Marcus growled.

"But…" Sara protested.

"The county is breathing down my back. The school board signed the contract for the new system over six months ago, but Dave still hasn't started. I realize he hadn't planned on being his dad's caregiver, but at some point, he has to do his job if he wants to continue to get paid. The community has only so much patience. Subject closed."

Jane stood. "I'm sorry to interrupt, Marcus, but we had a meeting set up for 9 a.m. Do you still have a minute to talk? I'm tying up all the loose ends of our choir trip."

Marcus looked up as if noticing Jane for the first time. "Of course, Jane. Sorry to keep you waiting. Come on in." His voice was still strained. "Please sit." He opened a yellow folder and pulled out the paper inside. "Hmmmm, you need charter bus confirmations from me. Anything else?" Marcus glanced at his watch as though in a hurry to move on.

"Were you able to book rooms for us for Saturday night? The competition ends after dinner on Saturday, and we all agreed that we'd rather spend the night in Virginia Beach than travel back to Crooked Run that late at night."

"Rooms confirmed, but not transportation yet. Now, all we need is a sure ticket to win."

"We're giving it our best shot."

"I saw Bethel at the grocery store the other day. There's no doubt in her mind Trinity Choir will win the first-place trophy, but she mentioned it would be nice if we landed second place, considering the tragedy with Clarence. She believes it would be a suitable tribute to his hard work if we were to win something."

"How generous of her," said Jane wryly. "It sounds as though the logistical pieces are coming together. Thank you for taking care of that."

"Oh, one snafu," said Marcus, "since that Brit guy came into the picture late, he will need to share a room with someone. Brad said he didn't mind."

Jane nodded.

"So if you see him, ask him if he's okay sharing."

"I'm sure he will be," said Jane. "I'm grateful he is helping."

"It's kind of weird how he just shows up."

Jane shook her head. "His story seemed pretty straightforward to me. He was at a turning point in his life–retirement, no commitments–and Emily asked him to return to the United States with her. So he sort of came on a whim."

"Pretty big life change to do on a whim."

"Sometimes it's good to be spontaneous," said Jane. "Now, one more thing before I go. It's getting chilly in the evenings now. And that man, Jax, is camping out in our town."

"Right now, he's camping out in the jail cell upstairs. Smith says forensics evidence reports will come in today. He's confident that this Jax had something to do with Clarence's murder."

Jane frowned. "It would surprise me if that were the case,"

"I wish I had your faith in humankind."

"Let's suppose for a moment that I'm right. We can't let Jax stay outside all winter. What provisions does Crooked Run have for the homeless?"

"Well, we haven't had that issue to deal with as far as I can remember. And frankly, I don't know how it's the town's fault the man doesn't have a place to stay."

"I'm not trying to imply the town is to blame. Shouldn't basic Christian charity make us want to help?"

Marcus shook his head. "I can bring it up at the next town council meeting, but I'm not sure many people will sympathize with the man. After all, we didn't ask him to come here on his crazy mission. It was his idea to trek across the country and land here in Crooked Run."

"I'm not going to judge the sanity of his actions. I'm saying that I don't think it's right to let him suffer in the cold all winter. I heard we can have some pretty heavy snow here in this part of the country."

"As I mentioned, Jane, I'll bring it up to the other council members, but at the moment, I can't come up with a solution. I suppose he can hang out in the library during the day."

"But the nights are the issue. They won't let Jax stick around the library overnight. What about one of the Sunday School rooms at church? Would it be possible for him to stay there?"

"You'd have to take that up with Rev. Bernard. I'm not sure the elders and the board of deacons would go for that. He's a stranger. Who knows what he would do? Steal money from the offering plate?"

Jane signed. "If the church can't help him, then who can?"

"Don't worry about it, Jane. If he's smart, he'll hitchhike back out west. Or who knows? Maybe a long-lost relative will show up."

Jane stood to leave. She wasn't getting anywhere with Marcus. She'd have to come up with a solution on her own. "Thank you for setting up the details for the trip. I guess I'll see you at the next practice?"

"I'll be there," said Marcus, rising. "We might show Bethel we're too good for a second-place trophy. We're sounding better now, thanks to your leadership."

"It's a group effort," said Jane. "I'm not doing it on my own."

She waved to Sara as she passed through the waiting room. The sound of voices came from the foyer. Chief Smith and Deputy Brad Harris were escorting a man to the door. It was Jax. So, the forensics report didn't implicate him in Clarence's murder. He was innocent - just like she believed. Jane nodded to the group as they passed by. Deputy Harris handed Jax his backpack and a small, fast food bag. At least they had given him lunch.

***

Cold air moved in, and the sky was overcast. A storm hovered on the horizon, and snow was on the way.

Jane had an idea taking shape in her mind. At first, she'd rejected the notion she might have a solution to Jax's winter housing problem. But just like the decision to lead the choir for the music competition, this idea was time-sensitive. She didn't have the luxury of mulling it over and studying it from all sides. Jax needed help how. This wouldn't wait. She said a quick prayer that she was doing the right thing and headed toward the Fairchild house. Implementing her plan would take more than a phone call.

As she pulled into the driveway, Jane saw the garden shed in the back. Despite its age and peeling paint, the building appeared sturdy and well-insulated. The Fairchilds had employed several full-time gardeners in the past, but that had been many years ago. Now, weeds grew alongside carefully planted bulbs, and wild roses were as plentiful as the hybrid bushes.

Lillie answered the door, her face and hands covered in flour. Lillie was always covered in something—paint, garden dirt, or flour.

"Did I interrupt baking day?" asked Jane, glad to be out of the biting wind and into the warm, fragrant kitchen.

"I'm trying my hand at flatbread." Lillie wiped her hands on her skirt, sending lines of white from the waistband to the hem. "Emily says we must expand our food horizons and eat more ethnic meals."

"It smells fantastic." Jane moved near to the kitchen table. "May I sit?"

"Of course! But I'm finished with the mixing part now, and I must wait an hour for the dough to rise. Let's go into the parlor and relax. I'll call Emily and Vada."

Jane wondered if Jasper was at home. She'd forgotten to check the garage to see if the sedan was parked there.

"Vada, Emily," Lillie called. "We have a visitor!"

The other two Fairchild sisters came from different parts of the house. They were delighted to see her.

"Jane, what a pleasant surprise!" said Vada, dropping onto the sofa.

"Thank you! I hope I haven't disturbed you."

"I was folding towels; I can do that anytime."

"I was brushing up on Edgar Allen Poe," said Emily. "The TellTale Heart always gives me such joy."

Jane laughed. "I wouldn't call a lunatic murdering an old man and hiding his dismembered corpse under the floor planks a joyful story."

"It's all in semantics. I sent Jasper to the store to buy some watercolors. I am thinking about starting painting lessons next week. The library is offering a class for beginners. I'm much more advanced than that, but one must take opportunities when they open up."

"Indeed," said Jane.

"Now Jane," said Vada, "we are ever so glad you are here for a visit, but I can't help but wonder if you have a more pressing reason for getting out on such a chilly day."

Jane nodded. "Very wise, Vada." She hesitated, then continued. "Do you remember the homeless man we've seen around town? The one we were talking about the other day?"

"You mean the crazy man who is always going on about his mission and the Lord's work?" said Emily.

Vada snorted, "Now that's not very kind, Emily. For all we know, he is doing God's work."

"The Lord wouldn't be so pushy." Emily scowled at her sister.

Jane continued, "As you are aware, he doesn't have a place to stay out of the cold, and the weather people are calling for freezing temperatures and snow this week."

89

Lillie nodded. "Jasper got us a week's worth of groceries in case we get snowed in."

"Lillie, you know we can't get snowed in. We can walk to the store if we need to." Vada shook her head.

"You don't remember the snow of '92, do you? It was so deep we couldn't even open the front door. The store was closed for three days."

"We won't have four feet of snow in November," said Vada.

"Ladies," said Jane, "if you'll allow me to continue?"

"Sorry," the three sisters said in unison.

"Now, back to Jax. As I said, he has nowhere to stay out of the cold. He can go to the library during the day - assuming they are open–but when they close, he has to return to his makeshift camp under the bridge at the park. And you know that if there is moisture in the ground, any precipitation will cause the river bottom to flood."

The ladies nodded. "That's a terrible situation," said Vada.

"What crossed my mind," said Jane, quickly before she lost her nerve, "is that perhaps you would find it in your hearts to allow him to stay in your garden shed. It looks well-built and insulated. I can bring over a space heater and a cot. It's not the Ritz, but at least he won't freeze."

Vada looked doubtful. "But is it safe? Isn't he a suspect in Clarence Jackson's death?"

Jane shook her head. "Not any longer. I was at the town office this morning when they released him. He looked so hopeless, clutching his lunch bag and knowing that the only place he could go was back under the bridge in the park."

"I know how judgmental the police force can be," said Emily. "One day, I'll tell you about my experience with murder back in England."

"Emily," said Lillie, "stop making everything about you. This poor man doesn't have a place to stay, and a storm is coming. I, for one, think we should let him live in our garden shed. He's annoying, but the last time I checked, that's not a sin."

"We have Jasper here to keep us safe if he gets out of hand," said Emily.

"Well," said Vada, "if you consider him harmless, I am fine with allowing him to stay in the shed. There is a large room and a smaller room. It would be best to set him up in the smaller section. It will be easier to keep it heated."

"I can bring over some vegetable soup for him this evening," said Jane. "I'll try to keep up with his meals since it was my idea to let him stay there."

"Don't worry about meals," Vada said. "It won't be any trouble to fix extra and take it to him. The poor man deserves home-cooked food once in a while."

"You ladies are angels." Jane smiled. "May I go to the shed and get a place ready for him?"

"Of course," said Lillie. "We'll all go with you. We have some old quilts we haven't used in a while. We can also give him an electric coffee pot," she continued, getting into the spirit of the adventure. "And I'll leave some books and magazines."

"I'm so glad the place has electricity," said Jane. "I'll bring over a card table and a folding chair."

"We'll set him up a regular little garden shed apartment," said Lillie.

The ladies grabbed their coats and started out the back door. A few snowflakes swirled in the wind, and the sky became leaden gray.

"We'll fix up the room. You go pick up Jax and bring him here. It won't take too long to have everything shipshape."

***

Jane found Jax huddled around a small fire, clutching a styrofoam cup. He stood up as he saw her approach his makeshift camp.

"Hello, Jax. Bad weather out here."

Jax nodded. "The storm is coming. Look at the clouds."

"You're right, Jax. Why don't you gather your belongings and come with me back to my car? I have some things to discuss with you."

He looked confused. "It's okay, Jax. It's me, Jane, from the church. We have found you a place to stay while you are here."

"No, don't take me to the state prison!" he shouted. He looked like he was about to run away.

Jane lowered her voice and talked to Jax gently as though she were talking to a young child.

"We're not taking you to jail, Jax. You're innocent. You're a free man. But look around you. See the snowflakes falling? It will probably snow a lot more this evening. You can't live here with no shelter. The Fairchild sisters said you can stay in their garden shed."

The old man looked like he understood their conversation for the first time. "A place for me?"

"Yes, Jax, a place for you. They are setting it up now. You'll have a bed, a coffee pot, some quilts, and some books and magazines to read."

The man's eyes filled with tears. "I was certain my time had come. I was sure I would freeze to death tonight."

Jane found her own eyes were wet. "No, Jax, there are still kind people left in the world. Now, gather up your belongings and come with me to the car. I'll drive you over and help you settle in. Miss Vada said she has some extra vegetable soup for you, and Miss Lillie is making bread. Nourishing food for a cold winter's night."

Jane opened the hatchback and tossed in the man's few belongings. The snow was coming down harder now. She hoped to settle Jax and return home before the roads got too bad. She turned up the thermostat in the car, and Jax sank into the heated leather seats. In a few moments, his eyes closed, and he was fast asleep.

Chapter 12

Jane held the phone away from her ear as Marcus's angry voice came through the other end.

"I hope the rumors I've heard are not true. I hope you have more sense than that!"

Jane sighed and looked out her living room window. The world already looked like a winter wonderland. Delicate snowflakes danced in the air as they fell gracefully to the ground. Earlier that morning, the precipitation had been heavier and thicker, but by midday, it had settled into a gentle pattern, turning the outside world into a peaceful snow globe. The glistening frost covered the rooftops, and a lacy fringe of white outlined the bare branches of the trees.

"Jane! Are you listening to me?"

The mayor's loud words jarred her back to reality. "What are you talking about, Marcus?" She was sure she understood what had prompted this phone call, but she wanted to hear his version.

"What am I talking about?" he growled. "I am talking about the fact you have sent a dangerous man to live with three helpless women. The fact you gave him food and a bed. Heck, you probably drained your bank account and gave him all your money, too."

"Marcus, stop." Jane's voice was gentle but firm. "If you remember correctly, I asked you about shelter for Jax earlier. And if you recall, you mentioned it would be impossible to find a place for him to stay."

"That's the truth," said Marcus. "We don't have accommodations for homeless, jobless people. Everybody in Crooked Run works. They have places to stay. And if they don't, they have families to help them out.

Nobody depends on the town to feed and shelter them."

"That's right," said Jane. "But listen to what you said. The people in Crooked Run have jobs. They have houses. They have a family. Jax has no one."

"And whose fault is that? Nobody asked him to move here. No one forced him to leave his home and hitchhike to Virginia. He made his own choices. The town of Crooked Run shouldn't feel obligated to help him."

"Marcus," said Jane. "Step outside. Tell me how long you could survive in this weather. Now settle down and listen to me. First, Jax isn't dangerous. Chief Smith found no evidence to link him to the murder of Clarence. He released him."

Marcus grunted, but he didn't interrupt her.

"Also, the ladies are not on their own. Jasper Reaves lives with them. He's a retired Scotland Yard Detective. If anyone can keep them safe, it's Jasper. Now, I don't know what kind of religion you practice or what moral code you follow, but I am unaware of any teachings that advocate allowing your fellow man to freeze to death in a snowstorm if you have the means to help him."

"You're on a high and mighty horse, Jane," said Marcus. "Just wait until he robs the Fairchild sisters blind. Just wait until he takes their money and leaves for the West Coast. Then who will have done the charitable thing?"

"Marcus, I know we will never agree on this subject. That is all I have to say. Other than your concern for the Fairchild sisters, this is none of your business. I heard of a need and did everything I could to take care of it. I am convinced that I saved a life."

"Jane, you can pretend to be the Good Samaritan all you want, but this matter is not settled. As a fellow choir member, I will let it rest for now. We both agree that winning this competition is the most important thing, and I don't want anything to get in the way. But trust me, Jane, this subject is not closed."

"Goodbye, Marcus. I hope you'll be at rehearsal on Monday evening. Of course, we'll cancel this evening's practice because of the snow."

But he had already rung off.

***

Jax stretched his legs in front of the space heater and looked around the cozy room. Apart from a pair of utility gloves and a rake in the corner, nothing showed this was a garden shed. A clean but threadbare rug covered the floor, and the walls were whitewashed. The Fairchild sisters had done a marvelous job of making the small room cozy. The garden shed was by far the nicest among all the places he had ever stayed.

Outside, the wind whistled and shook the gigantic oak trees around the shed. Snow had drifted almost to the low window. He wouldn't have made it on his own. They would have dug his frozen body out of the snow. He hadn't expected snow in November. He would have made better plans if he had. Jax was used to being outdoors but didn't have the equipment for weather like this. He closed his eyes and wondered again if he'd misunderstood the message.

He'd heard the phone call and the human message, all right. That part was simple. The human had tracked him down at the library one hot August day when the heat was unbearable outside. The call was quick and to the point. Jax wondered, though, if the message was from God as well. He'd prayed and listened to answers for three days straight. He was sure God said 'yes.' Now, he was uncertain. His missions had never led him on such an arduous journey before. The call and the response always matched. Something went wrong this time. They accused him of taking another's life. And he'd almost died in this storm. What had he done wrong?

But the huge bowl of vegetable soup and the thick slices of homemade bread were comforting, and his eyelids drooped. He'd have to consider this dilemma later. He lay on the cot and pulled the quilt over his thin frame. Jax dozed off to sleep, snug and well-fed for the first time in many days.

***

Chief Smith stared gloomily out his office window. The snow fell heavier now, and the wind whipped around the eaves of the building. He was no farther along on the Clarence Jackson murder case than he'd been five days ago. He should call in the state police again. After their initial visit, he'd assured them he had the situation well under control and that he'd already apprehended the person who was most likely the killer. But it all turned upside down. Jax was not his man. Pure and simple. He had no involvement in the crime. Nothing linked him to the case.

Smith was a little ashamed of himself for profiling the homeless man. He wouldn't have taken anybody else in for questioning with so little evidence. And now, he was paying for his mistake. He'd wasted time while the actual killer was still out there.

The town council members were getting antsy, too. They were working on an extensive tourism campaign with several neighboring towns. "Nobody is going to want to visit Crooked Run with an unsolved murder hanging over our heads," Reggie Reynolds, the chair, said. Smith wasn't sure if anybody would visit Crooked Run without a murder, either. The town didn't offer many tourist attractions.

The blizzard wasn't making it any easier. Most of the roads were too slippery to risk driving on today. Nobody in their right mind would travel in this storm, anyway. He wondered if he should close the office early and head for home. He'd already dismissed Deputy Harris for the day. Brad lived outside Crooked Run on a country road, and Smith knew it would soon be impassable. The chief had spent nights at the office before, but they were not restful times.

He glanced again at the paper with the cutout magazine letters. His only clue. That and Dave's wrench. And he was 99% sure the young sound technician didn't kill the choir director.

If he had carefully considered it, he would have also realized that a homeless man wouldn't have easy access to scissors, glue, magazines, and paper. And if he had used the library to create the note, someone would have seen him. Those kinds of messages were so difficult to track. Clarence had left countless fingerprints on it, but the lab couldn't pick up any other prints. Someone had also wiped the amp and the electric panel box clean.

Smith found it hard to believe that nobody saw anyone enter the church after choir Thursday evening or early Friday morning. No one had seen Clarence or his killer. Or so they said. He believed that small towns always had someone who saw everything. The one time he wished Olive Thomas was watching, she was oblivious to her surroundings.

He heard a car skid through the parking lot and saw the red Lexus spinning onto the street. Marcus was leaving early, too. He'd sent Sara back as soon as she came in this morning. Now, Smith was the only one in the building. The chief signed his name to several more documents. He might as well go home. He could worry about the case just as well in his recliner as in this uncomfortable office chair.

He turned out the lights and reached for his keys.

***

Gloria Jackson sat in front of the small hotel window and watched the snow fall. She hoped the weather would clear up for Clarence's service. She wasn't interested in staying in Crooked Run any longer than she had to. The police had given the go-ahead for the funeral on Sunday.

She was still stunned by the amount of money Clarence had left her. Where did his windfall of cash come from? And why did he leave it to her?

She had hoped the sealed letter in the will documents would explain where Clarence's money had come from and why he'd left it to her. But she was disappointed to find the envelope contained a single sheet of paper with a short poem written in Clarence's bold block letters.

In life's unfolding tale, where once we intertwined,
I leave you now this legacy, though we've left love behind.
Not in regret or lingering pain, do I give this wealth to thee,
But in gratitude for what we shared, in moments, you and me.
Through days of laughter, nights of tears, we journeyed side by side,

Yet paths diverged, as fate decreed, our love did not abide,
But know this gift is not for loss, nor for the past's refrain,
It's for the strength you showed, my dear, through joy and even pain.

What there some cryptic message she was supposed to figure out? She doubted it. Clarence often acted on a whim.

The hotel phone buzzed. She answered it. Someone was in the lobby to see her. Someone she had hoped to never run into again.

***

By Saturday morning, the snow had stopped, and a bright November sun pushed away the clouds. Jane woke early. The hospitality committee was meeting at the fellowship hall to prepare food for Clarence's funeral meal, and she had to get there first to unlock the door. She and Anne needed to go over special music for Thanksgiving as well. She had to keep better track of the liturgical calendar.

When Jane arrived at the church fellowship hall, Martha Jones and three other hospitality committee members were waiting at the door. They all carried crock pots, casserole dishes, and iced tea jugs. None of them looked happy.

"Good thing it didn't start snowing again," said Martha, glaring at Jane. "There's one thing you need to know about the folks in Crooked Run: we are not layabouts. When there's a job to be done, we get up early and do it!"

I'm so sorry, Mrs. Jones. Nobody told me what time you were meeting. I thought 8:00 would be early enough.

"I get up at 4:00 every morning," said the head deacon's wife, Evie Reynolds. "Day's half done by 8:00."

"Only if you go to bed at noon," Jane wanted to say but smiled through her irritation. By the looks of the paraphernalia the women carried, they'd already prepared the food.

The fellowship hall was soon a buzz of activity. Scents wafting from the kitchen were a curious mix of cleaning products and jalapeño poppers. The women unfolded long plastic tables and set them up in a U shape along the sides of the room.

"What kind of decorations should we put on the tables, Martha?" asked a young red-haired girl, clearly in training.

"Grab those magnolia blossoms out of the storage closet. We don't want to be too festive. It is a funeral meal, after all."

"Has anybody heard if they have any suspects in Clarence's murder yet?" asked Evie. "Olive told me that your Pete found the body, Martha."

"You leave my Pete out of this!" Martha put her hands on her hips and frowned at the deacon's wife. "That Olive had better mind her own business."

97

Evie's face turned red. "I'm simply making conversation, Martha. Not accusing Pete of anything wrong."

But Martha had already moved back into the kitchen.

Chapter 13

Rev. Barnard suggested they hold Clarence's service at the Crooked Run Funeral home rather than at the church. They would have a post funeral meal back in the Fellowship Hall. Jane and the deacons agreed. It wasn't proper to eulogize a man in the same spot where he was murdered. They had already made the arrangements before discovering that Clarence had a living next of kin. Or at least an ex-next of kin. Gloria Jackson was pleasant enough, but it didn't seem to matter to her where and how they conducted Clarence's funeral.

The handful of Crooked Run citizens who turned out to mourn Clarence did not fill half of the chairs. An eerie quietness hung in the air. Olive Thomas wiped her eyes with a crumpled tissue, leaving everyone to guess whether her tears were for the deceased or for show. Her neighbors counted on her for a detailed account of the events.

"Is that her?" asked Emily. Her voice sounded like a shout in the stillness.

"Shhh!" hissed Vada. In a hushed whisper, she continued, "Yes, that is Clarence's ex. Now stop talking, and for heaven's sake, turn around! She can hear you, you know."

Anne played the opening measure of "Amazing Grace," and the congregation settled back to enjoy the music.

Jane began the service with a prayer and a formal obituary reading. Rev. Barnard came up next to deliver the eulogy. He cleared his throat and looked out over the congregation.

"Friends," he began, "Today, we come together to say goodbye to a man who may have caused conflicting emotions in our lives but whose influence on our community cannot be overlooked.

"As we honor the memory of our late choir director, Mr. Clarence Jackson, we should reflect upon the musical blessings he shared with us in the few months he was part of our congregation. Mr. Jackson possessed a sincere dedication to the art of choral music. His unwavering commitment to excellence was clear in his countless hours helping us refine our voices and guiding us through difficult musical scores. While his methods may have been stern, his relentless pursuit of perfection challenged us to strive to do our best."

Lillie cleared her throat loudly, and Vada put a finger to her lips to shush her.

Rev. Barnard continued. "In his role as our director, Mr. Jackson demanded nothing short of excellence, and for that, we are grateful. He held us to the highest standards, never content with mediocrity, and in doing so, he cultivated within us a deep appreciation for the beauty of music and the power of collective harmony."

"Collective cacophony, if you ask his professor buddy," whispered Emily. Vada gave her sister a dirty look.

"As we bid farewell to Mr. Clarence Jackson, let us remember him for his formidable talent as a musician and for the indelible mark he left upon our hearts and souls. Rest in peace, Mr. Jackson. May your melodies echo eternally in the halls of our memories."

Outside, the wind whispered through the trees, as if even nature was unsure how to mourn a man who wasn't well-liked. And as they lowered the casket to the ground, they heard a distant wail of a siren fading into the air like a melancholy farewell.

     ***

Gloria Jackson did not stay for the post-funeral meal, yet Jane felt obliged to visit her at the hotel before Clarence's ex-wife went back to her home. She wasn't sure what she'd say to Gloria, but she could at least read some scriptures and offer a prayer.

The Waypoint Inn wasn't the Ritz, but it was clean and cheerful. The foyer was decorated for autumn. Real cornstalks were tied together to form a backdrop for a cascade of pumpkins, winter squash, and gourds. The young receptionist greeted Jane as if she were the customer of the day.

"How may I help you, ma'am?" Jane wouldn't have been surprised if she had curtsied.

"I'm here to meet Ms. Gloria Jackson. I don't know her room number."

"Over here," came a voice from a table by the window. A stout woman dressed in a fuchsia sweater motioned her over. "Coffee's passable. I wouldn't recommend the hot chocolate or tea, though. Too watery."

"Gloria Jackson?" Jane recognized their late choir director's wife from seeing her at Clarence's funeral.

"The same. Although, why I keep Clarence's last name is a mystery, even to me. Old habits, I guess. Have a seat, Rev. Cartwright."

"Just Jane." Jane removed her jacket and hung it on the back of her chair. The hotel café was delightfully cozy and inviting.

"Thanks for stopping by. The funny thing is, you probably knew Clarence better than I did. We have been separated for over forty years."

"I'm new here," said Jane as a young server filled her upturned coffee mug. "Clarence was our choir director for a short time. I am so sorry for your loss."

Gloria shrugged. "I'm surprised they tracked me down to let me know Clarence was dead. Murdered. Can you believe it? You'd think this little place would be on America's safest town list."

"Evil doesn't discriminate. I think it was Agatha Christie who said, 'There is evil everywhere under the sun.'"

"What surprises me more than anything is the chunk of money Clarence left me. He didn't have two nickels to rub together when we were married. I would love to know where he got so much cash." Gloria dumped a generous amount of sugar into her cup and stirred. "And the biggest shock is why he left it to me."

"Does he have any other living relatives?"

"I don't think so. He was an only child, and his parents died in a car crash soon after we were married. I'm not surprised that I'm the only living acquaintance. I'm curious why he didn't leave the money to one of his music charities, though. Or why he didn't create a scholarship in his name at his beloved Julliard."

"That is strange," said Jane. "Maybe he still had feelings for you. The heart sometimes has a mind of its own."

"Are you married, Rev.?" asked Gloria.

"Widowed," said Jane. "I lost my husband in a drowning accident four years ago. He was trying to save a young boy in our youth group. He got pulled under by a riptide."

"Forgive me if this sounds harsh, but did they recover his body?"

Jane nodded. "They were able to revive him, and he lived for a few hours."

"I'm sorry, Rev. My brother died similarly. We never found him, though."

"Oh, that's awful. I am so sorry."

Both women sat in silence for a few moments until Gloria said, "But enough sadness. I appreciate you coming to visit today. Actually, I was going to call you anyway. I'd like to pay for the church roof repair."

Jane stared at the woman. "What? Pay for the roof? That will cost a lot of money. The insurance claim produced little cash. They said we'd been neglectful in keeping up with general repairs."

Gloria looked out the window, a slight smile on her face. "I feel like I owe old Clarence something. We had a few good months. I think he'd be happy with my contribution to the church."

"I don't know what to say, Ms. Jackson. I'm overwhelmed."

"No need to say anything. Do you have a card with the church's contact information?"

Jane nodded, still shocked by the woman's generous offer.

Gloria stood. "Thanks. I'll be in touch. And thank you for stopping by to visit. You didn't have to do that."

Jane took the other woman's hand. "Thank you. And please, come back to visit us soon."

Gloria shook her head. "No, I don't think so. There are some people in your town I would be happy never to see again. Goodbye, Rev., and take care."

Chapter 14

Jane was amazed to see that the inside of the church looked the same as it always had. She wasn't sure what she expected, but violent death should have left some disturbance in the tranquil atmosphere. But the same muted light filtered in the windows, and the same musty scent of congregations long past lingered in the air. A construction team had patched the ceiling where the speaker had once hung, and a new amplifier with a fresh-looking cord was on the stage—the only changes in the sanctuary.

Chief Smith's morning call informing her that the choir had permission to practice in the sanctuary again took her by surprise, but she was grateful. Although the first rehearsal back on the church stage might be awkward, it somehow seemed fitting. The sooner they settled back into their routine, the better. With the competition date looming, tension was high.

The sound of angry voices interrupted her thoughts. Someone was in the music storage room. Strange. She was sure she was alone.

"I've already lied for you once. Why do you keep asking me to do more?" the female voice sounded bitter.

"Isn't this relationship worth a few bumps in the road?" asked a male voice.

"This situation is more than a bump in the road. Besides, my divorce isn't final yet. I don't want anything to get in the way of the settlement. I can't afford to live on what I make at the flower shop."

"Money over love. A typical female response." The male sounded disgusted.

"It's not like you can afford to keep going the way you're headed. Your dad's insurance covers some things, but you must also shell out a lot of your money. And he's not able to work. He may never have the physical ability to farm again."

"That's exactly why I need to follow through with this."

"No. It's too dangerous. You'll need to come up with something else if you want me to go along with it."

Jane moved to the back of the sanctuary to avoid eavesdropping on the rest of the conversation. She recognized the voices: Dave Harper and Anne Farmer. Curiosity tempted her to stay, but her courtesy and good sense urged her to go. Besides, it was nearly time for rehearsal, and the others would be here soon.

As if on cue, the outside door to the fellowship hall swung open, and the Fairchild sisters came in, their scarves blown about their faces and their hair tossed in scarecrow fashion. Jasper followed several paces behind, calm and unruffled as usual. These days, Emily relied less and less on her walking stick or Jasper's arm. This suave Englishman had worked more than one miracle in the few weeks he'd been in town.

"You can't join now," said Vada. "They have the list posted and have already printed the programs."

"But I'm familiar with the song. I sang Ave Maria at St. Paul's Cathedral in London. Surely, I can sing it in a dumpy little competition."

"Jane will have the final say," said Lillie, panting as she tried to keep up with her sisters. "But don't be mad if you have to sit it out."

"I'm a soprano, and I suspect that's a weak area," Emily said, looking directly at Vada. "What if I changed my name to Vada? They would never know."

"Don't go there," warned Vada.

"Ladies, so good to see you!" Jane welcomed the bickering sisters. "Did you say you're a soprano, Emily?"

"A coloratura soprano," said Emily.

"A what?" asked Lillie, turning around to look at her sister.

"The highest form of soprano, sister dear. I can reach notes nobody else can manage."

"We have already registered our choir, Emily," said Jane. "I wish we could include you, but it's too late to add members. I can contact Bethel this evening to confirm, but I believe they've already finished the rosters."

"Told you!" Vada smirked.

"But," said Jane, "We'd love to have you join our Harmony church choir. Your high soprano voice would be a true asset."

Emily scowled and took a seat in the front row. "We'll see about that."

The other choir members trickled in now. Anne sat at the piano, and Dave was in the choir's back row. Somewhere amid the hustle and bustle of the Fairchild sisters' arrival, they had finished their argument—or at least put it on hold—and had slipped back into their spots. Sara and Marcus were the only choir members not yet in place.

Jane stepped behind the podium. "So nice to see everyone, and I'm glad to be back in our usual practice spot. Even though it's strange in some ways, it's good for us to be in familiar territory. We are just a short time away from the big day. I am very pleased with our progress."

The group murmured in agreement.

Shortly after Jane motioned for the choir to stand, Marcus rushed in, followed by Sara. Both were flushed and hurried into their places without looking at each other.

Anne started the introduction again, and the choir began to sing. Emily joined in from the front row. Despite scowls from her sisters, she continued singing - raising her voice louder on the high notes.

Jane tried her best not to let Clarence's less-than-flattering notes about the singers color her judgment, but he was often spot-on with his observations. Choir directing was a delicate balance between keeping the music on pitch and trying not to hurt anyone's feelings.

One of the last skills the choir had to master was breath control. The phrases in Ave Maria were long and lyrical, requiring the singers to maintain consistent breath support. Jane struggled to pace the song so the choir could breathe but still sustain the phrases effectively, but they were almost there.

"Wonderful job, folks!" Jasper smiled at the group. "You've got this! Now go home, get rest, and pamper your vocal chords. Drink tea with lemon and honey. And don't strain your voice. Save it for the big day."

"And don't shout or scream," said Lillie. "And take your allergy medicine," she added.

"Yes, thank you for those helpful tips, Miss Fairchild," said Jasper. "Just a few more days, and we can show the rest of the world the results of our hard work."

Jane nodded. "Next practice, we'll do a dress rehearsal. I should have the robes dry-cleaned by then." She dismissed the singers. "Drive safely, and we'll meet again on Friday night."

"Nice job–as always, Director." Jasper touched Jane on the shoulder as he passed by.

"Thank you, Director," said Jane. "Teamwork!"

The choir members filed out, and Jane stayed behind to ensure the lights were off. It had been a solid practice, and she was pleased with how the group worked together. She noticed Dave lingering behind, fiddling with a knob on the new amplifier.

"That back section sounds nice, Dave. You guys have learned to blend your voices well."

He nodded. "You're doing a super job directing us. And you don't yell."

"I try not to. By the way, how's your dad doing?"

"I think he might be getting a little better. I wish he'd do what the doctor tells him to."

"Most men are difficult patients," she smiled. "Please give him my best. I'll try to get over to visit him this week."

"Thank you, Rev. Cartwright. You can go ahead; I'll lock up. I have a few things I need to check out with the sound system."

"Thank you," said Jane. She could not resist glancing around for Anne. The pianist had already left.

***

Jane poured a cup of hot chocolate and settled down to relax from the long day. So much had happened in the past few weeks, and she had so little time to process it all. The incident with the speaker, Clarence's murder, Emily and Jasper's arrival, Jax, and the snow. She'd be glad when the competition was over. Even if she decided to direct the Harmony church choir on a more permanent basis, she would take a rest first. The choir needed a break as well. They had worked hard. She wasn't sure why, but she hadn't mentioned Gloria Jackson's offer to pay for the new church roof to anyone. But there would be plenty of time to talk about it if Gloria did, indeed, send the money.

Rev. Barnard had hinted that he wanted her to lead Sunday services after the first of the year. She knew some congregation members would not be happy with his decision. But she wouldn't try to change their minds. Either they'd accept her, or they would find another church. Although that was easy to say, she was hurt by the fact some congregation members believed she was in the wrong career.

A siren's piercing wail broke through the night. Red and blue lights flashed through her window. She felt a pang of dread. Had one of the choir members been in an accident on the way home? Immediately, she chided herself for her negative thoughts.

Her phone rang.

"Jane, it's Vada. Come over here quickly. Jax is missing."

"What do you mean, missing?"

"I went to take him a snack, and the garden shed was empty. His clothes are gone, and the dishes are all stacked by the door."

"Did you call the police?" asked Jane.

"No, Jasper said he hasn't been gone long enough to be considered a missing person."

"I saw the ambulance and police cars passing my house a few moments ago."

"There was a big pileup on the Interstate. Emily has a scanner."

"I'll come over, but I'm not sure how much help I'll be," said Jane.

"We're going to form a search party to find him. Chief Smith might think I'm crazy, but I believe Jax is in danger."

***

Chief Smith pulled the cruiser behind the ambulance's flashing red lights. The scene did not look good. A contorted twist of metal connected the guardrail's side with the black Tesla's front. Debris littered the asphalt and shattered glass fragments glinted in the emergency lights like scattered diamonds. The air was heavy with the scent of burnt rubber and fuel, a tangible reminder of the violent force that had brought the vehicle to its abrupt halt.

A makeshift tent covered the driver's side, confirming Chief Smith's fears that the driver had not escaped the crash alive.

"It's a bad one, Chief." A paramedic walked up to join Smith. "Looks like she lost control of the car. It seems to me that she didn't make an effort to stop.

"Alcohol involved?"

"I can't confirm it, but I'd guess that was the case."

"Any idea who it is?"

"Her driver's license says Gloria Jean Jackson. Does the name sound familiar?"

Chief Smith groaned.

Chapter 15

The ground around the shed was muddy from the melting snow, and Jasper struggled to find any sign of footprints. The moon was a sliver, and the lack of light made detecting any detailed marks on the ground impossible.

"The day was so warm, he probably decided it was time to go back to living under the bridge," said Emily. "You never know with his type."

"What do you mean, 'his type'?" said Lillie, glowering at her sister. "Jax is a person like us. He's not a type. And he wouldn't leave without saying goodbye."

Jane pulled into the Fairchild's driveway and followed the line of flashlights behind the house. Usually, she wouldn't be concerned about a grown man who had moved on after the weather turned milder. Besides, she knew from his brief visit last week he could disappear quickly. But she had a nagging worry about all the strange things going on.

"Hello, ladies. Thanks for calling me."

"I didn't want to disturb you," said Emily. "But these two—" she pointed to her sisters — "insisted that we tell you."

"I'm glad you called," Jane repeated. "I feel responsible for Jax as well. I can't imagine him wandering off without telling anybody."

Lillie gave Emily a triumphant smirk. "Told you!"

Jane looked inside the building. The light was on, and somebody had turned off the space heater. Someone had also folded the quilt on the cot and stacked two bowls and a plate on the small card table by the door. It didn't look as though Jax had left in a hurry.

"His light was still on when we got home from choir practice, so I took

108

him some hot cocoa and a few chocolate chip cookies I'd baked this after-noon," Vada said. "The door was unlocked, but nobody was inside."

"I'll bet he went out for a moonlight stroll." Jane doubted her first impressions. After all, Jax was used to living alone and surviving without the comforts of home. It would have been polite for him to have told the sisters if he was moving on, but maybe he lived by a different code.

"It would still be a good idea to call Chief Smith," said Lillie. "I have an uneasy feeling about this."

Jasper shook his head. "Lillie, as far as Chief Smith can tell, nothing is wrong. Jax hasn't been missing more than four hours. You took him dinner before choir practice, right? He was here then?"

Lillie nodded. "Yes, He seemed the same as always. A little vague, but grateful for the food. I told him we were going to choir practice and wished him a good evening."

"So you didn't sense anything was amiss?" Jasper studied her face.

"No, nothing that stood out."

"It's getting chilly, ladies." Jasper pulled his jacket tighter. "The wind's picked up, and temperatures are dropping. You should go back inside now. I'll take another walk around the property and see if I can spot him any-where. Please try not to worry."

The ladies trudged back toward the house. Jane lingered behind.

"Do you suppose he's okay?" she asked. "Or were you trying to keep the sisters from worrying?"

"A little of both." Jasper broke a twig from a maple tree next to the shed and tossed it into the air. "On the surface, it seems ludicrous that we're concerned about a man who traveled across the country without transporta-tion. We all know in our minds that he can manage on his own. Our hearts, however, tell us otherwise."

Jane nodded. "I agree. Something is not right. But you're correct in saying that Chief Smith will not take us seriously. He's already sure that Jax had nothing to do with Clarence's murder, and solving that case is all that is consuming his mind now. He wouldn't invest time and personnel to search for a man who might simply have returned to his home out west."

"And possibly, that's what happened."

"Does that mean we stop looking for him and go about our daily lives? Assume he's okay?" Jane looked doubtful.

"I guess that would be the sensible thing to do," said Jasper. "But I don't always take the sensible route."

"Nor I," Jane admitted. "Perhaps we should start our own investigation. And if he did pack up and move on his own accord, nobody would know we played detective."

"That sounds like an excellent plan," said Jasper. "We can't do anything else tonight, but I'll talk with the mayor and Chief Smith tomorrow morning. I don't expect much help, but it's a place to start."

"I'll talk to Rev. Bernard and Dave Harper to check if Jax stopped by the church at any point. Jax loves to quote scripture. He may have some religious connections."

"Good point. Shall we meet up before choir practice to compare notes? Say, around lunch?"

"What about the Latte? Can you come around 1:00?"

"That sounds delightful," said Jasper.

"Good." Jane smiled

"I hope we're not on a fool's errand."

Jane nodded, but in her heart, she thought that a fool's errand—or any other errand—would not be a waste of time with such a handsome accomplice.

Chapter 16

Jasper was glad that Vada hadn't paid the water bill yet. It gave him a perfect excuse to visit the Town Office. He hoped to catch an informal word with Marcus rather than schedule a meeting with him. Jane had made it clear Marcus had little sympathy for Jax, and he was sure the mayor wouldn't care the homeless man was missing.

Jasper went out to recheck the shed before leaving to ensure Jax hadn't returned. The room was as they'd left it the night before, and he could see no sign the homeless man had returned during the night.

As he drove by Crooked Run Fellowship, Jasper noticed the custodian, Pete Jones, pulling weeds around the front steps. The town was returning to normal after their brief brush with sudden death. Or, to put it in more chilling terms, their brief brush with murder. He was mildly surprised that nobody in Crooked Run appeared unduly nervous about the possibility of a killer still on the loose. In his experience, though, most people didn't expect to be a victim of murder. Violent death was something on TV cop shows, not anything that happened in real life. He wondered if the murder would have made a more significant impact if anyone in town had liked Clarence.

He pulled the Fairchild's car between Marcus's red Lexus and a souped-up truck. The vehicles testified to the diversity of small-town personalities.

"May I help you?" The voice was close, and Jasper realized he'd walked into the office without noticing the woman at the desk. He wasn't sure how he'd missed Sara. Her light brown hair fell in loose curls past her shoulders, and her blue eyes were bright. He'd seen her at choir practice, but so many other things had been going on he hadn't realized how attractive she was.

"Good morning, ma'am. I'm Jasper Reaves. I'm here to pay the utility

111

bill for the Fairchild sisters."

"Please call me Sara. After all, we are fellow choir members."

"Well, if it isn't the Englishman. Hello, Jasper." Marcus came from his office carrying a large portfolio in one arm and a stack of folders in the other.

"Good morning, mayor. You look busy. Putting the taxpayers' money to good use, I see."

"I try." Marcus smiled. "It's only 9 a.m., and I've already completed and signed these grant proposals. Now it's up to Sara to mail them."

Sara sighed. "Just add it to my pile. I'll get out of here by midnight if I'm lucky."

"Since you're finished with your part, mayor, do you have a few minutes to spare?" asked Jasper.

Marcus nodded toward his office. "Sure, come on in."

The office was sparsely decorated. No pictures of family or friends, sports team posters, or paraphernalia provided any clues about Marcus's personality.

"What can I do for you, Mr. Englishman?" Marcus clicked his pen as though eager to move on.

"I wanted to update you on the man camping in the park. Jax. He appears to have left town."

Marcus drummed his fingers on the desk. "Right off the top of my head, I'd say that's a good thing."

"He is, of course, a free man who can travel when and where he wishes. It's unusual he would leave without telling the Fairchild sisters or Jane goodbye, though."

"Not unusual at all." Marcus swiveled his chair to face the window. "Those kinds of folks come and go as they please. No ties to family. No friends. No attachments. I'm not at all surprised he's gone."

"I didn't get the impression that he was in a hurry to leave. He seemed to be content in the garden shed. And, of course, the Fairchild sisters kept him comfortable and well-fed."

"Like I said, you can't figure out a pattern with homeless people. If I were you, I wouldn't make too much of it. He came, didn't like what he found, and he left. Simple as that." Marcus turned back around and opened his laptop.

"So, you don't suppose he had any connection with Clarence's death?"

Marcus's face became wary again. "Why do you say that? Smith cleared him, didn't he? And as badly as he wants to wrap up this case, it's clear he'd have held him if he had any evidence to go on."

"I suppose you're right," said Jasper, standing. "But if you hear anything of his whereabouts, please call me."

"Will do, sir." Marcus rose to shake Jasper's hand, but the mayor's eyes were on his computer.

Jasper stopped to tell Sara goodbye on his way out. She was deep in paperwork, so he didn't stay to chat, not that he wouldn't have liked to. He scolded himself for admiring her. She was at least twenty years younger than he was. And with his track record with women, he needed all the odds stacked in his favor.

Jasper's conversation with Chief Smith was like his talk with the mayor. Smith had little interest in the homeless man or his whereabouts. "I went out on a limb when I took him in for questioning," said Smith. "I wouldn't have held him if he hadn't requested to stay in the jail cell overnight because of the cold temperatures.

Jasper felt a pang of sorrow for Jax. It must be terrible to believe that a jail cell was the best place he could spend the night. "It's not my business, but do you have any leads on Jackson's murder?"

Smith shook his head. "An unaccounted-for wrench and a mysterious note. That's the extent of my evidence." He sighed and continued. "The state is sending in a detective. I suspect he will find the case as dry and clue-free as I do. Whoever killed Clarence knew what he was doing. Had the skill to bypass safety measures on the fuse box and knew how to cover his tracks."

"Some cases are never solved," said Jasper, recalling his days at the Yard.

"I hope this is not one of them." Chief Smith shook his head. "And now, things are even more complicated. There was a bad accident on the Interstate last night."

"I saw the rescue vehicles go past. I hope it wasn't anybody from Crooked Run."

Smith hesitated and ran a hand over his face. "Not exactly. But she did have connections to Crooked Run. The victim was Gloria Jackson. Clarence Jackson's ex."

Jasper whistled. "Is she going to be okay?"

Smith shook his head. "She didn't survive the impact."

***

Jane found Rev. Barnard in his back garden planting fall garlic bulbs. The elderly man rose and gave a slight bow. "I would greet you properly, but my hands are a mess." He wiped them on his black pants, creating ridges of dirt and mud on the polyester

"Sorry to bother you, Rev. Barnard. I can come back another time if you're busy."

"Never too busy for you, Jane. Why don't you go inside to the sun porch? I'll wash this dirt from my hands and make us some tea. Bertha

113

has the day off today, so I'll try my hand at boiling water." He beamed, his wrinkled face breaking into hundreds of crinkles.

Three overstuffed patio chairs and a comfortable-looking porch swing filled the small sunroom. Jane chose the swing. November had given them another rare, summer-like day. How frustrating it must be to predict the weather in the Shenandoah Valley. The mountains on either side had the potential to deflect a storm at a moment's notice.

Rev. Barnard went into the side kitchen door. She should have offered to help him, but the swing was too cozy and pleasant.

"Earl Grey or mint?" he called from the kitchen doorway.

"Mint, please. Is it from your garden?"

"Indeed," he said with an air of pride. "Grew it myself. Or I should say I allowed it to invade my garden. Mint sure has a will of its own."

Jane sipped the sweet drink and sighed. Few things matched the flavor of fresh garden tea. As C.S. Lewis said, "You can never have a cup of tea large enough or a book long enough to suit me."

Rev. Barnard sat on the chair nearest her and pulled over a small table for their teacups. "To what do I owe this pleasure?"

"I'd like to say I came to relax, drink tea, and discuss philosophy with you." Jane said, "But I'm afraid my visit is more complicated than that. What do you know about the homeless man, Jax?"

Rev. Barnard looked puzzled. "I don't know him at all. He never attended a church service, at least while I was there. I saw him sitting on the back pew several mornings when I came to pray. He looked deep in meditation, so I didn't bother him."

"He was in church?" That was new information.

"Yes. I saw him several days in a row. He may have been sitting inside to get out of the cold, but he had such a deep look of reverence on his face I didn't feel it would be appropriate to disturb him."

"Is Chief Smith aware of this?"

"Oh, of course. I called the police office right after I heard the news about Clarence."

Jane gave an inward sigh of relief. "I suppose he had no reason to suspect him of foul play then."

"I don't think Jax is capable of foul play," said Rev. Barnard. "He seemed to be a confused, rather lost soul."

"He appears to have left town." Jane weighed her words carefully.

"Oh? Is he headed back out west?"

"He didn't say. He just left. Disappeared without saying goodbye to anyone."

"Was he close enough to anyone to tell them his plans?"

114

"Probably not," said Jane. "The Fairchild sisters let him stay in their garden shed during that pop-up snowstorm at the start of the week. We thought he was comfortable there."

"But he left," said Rev. Barnard.

"Yes. After choir practice last night, Vada Fairchild went out to give him some hot cocoa and cookies and found the light on, but nobody was there."

"Did he take his things with him?"

"All he had was a dirty book bag and some odds and ends. Everything's gone."

Rev. Barnard looked thoughtful. "Now that is unusual. I don't suppose the authorities will look for him since, technically, he isn't 'missing.'"

"I have my doubts," agreed Jane. "But I'm worried that something is wrong."

"Don't dismiss feelings," said Rev. Barnard as he poured another cup of tea. "Care for more?"

"No, thank you, Rev. It was delicious, but I must be going."

"I'm sorry I wasn't much help. Please keep me updated if you find him. I will do the same."

"Thank you, Rev. Barnard. And thank you for the tea. It was heavenly!"

"The kind of tea you'd expect from a reverend, right?" His kind blue eyes twinkled.

***

Jane left Rev. Barnard's cottage, deep in thought. Even though Jax had, indeed, been in the sanctuary, she still couldn't see him as a murderer. She felt there was much more to Jax's story than she or anyone else in Crooked Run could fathom.

Although Dave's car was not in the garage, she stopped at the Harper house anyway. It wouldn't hurt to double-check. Besides, she'd promised to visit Mr. Harper earlier that week. She rang the doorbell.

"Dave's not here," said Zander Harper, maneuvering his wheelchair away from the door to allow Jane to enter.

"Sorry, I missed him." Jane smiled at Mr. Harper. He looked pale and gaunt. The accident had taken its toll on the once robust farmer.

"Would you like to stay awhile?" he asked. He motioned to a small sofa near the door.

"I'll sit a minute. I don't have a lot of time to visit. This choir competition is so demanding. We're so close to our performance."

"I guess you'll see Dave at choir practice," said Mr. Harper. "I'm sure he'll come home to cook dinner for me soon if you want to wait. Some day, I hope to have these counters lowered so I can be a bit more independent and fix my own meals. Dave said there are complete floor plans that convert conventional kitchens to make them more accessible."

That was a step in the right direction, Jane thought. "I'm amazed at what a talented carpenter can do to a place. We lived in an old farmhouse back in California. The kitchen was small and boxy, and the dining room was even tinier. We hired a construction team to tear out walls and put in more windows. The difference was incredible. Didn't look like the same house."

"Yeah, I wish we could afford to do something like that. This apartment didn't seem so small until I had to sit and stare at its four walls all day."

"Well, here's hoping you can get out and about soon. I know winter can be a difficult time. The days are so short."

"And the nights are so long," he added. "But, as my mom used to say, 'things could be worse.' Can I get you a drink or something?" He caught the meaning of his words and shook his head. "I guess I should have said drinks are in the fridge if you'd like one."

Jane smiled. "Thanks, but I came here from Rev. Barnard's place. He filled me to the brim with mint tea."

Mr. Harper nodded. "That Reverend is a devout man. He's been to see me every week since the accident. He doesn't mind when I rant and rave at a God who would let me end up in such a state."

Jane didn't want to discuss free will and misguided choices, so she simply smiled. This man had plenty to think about without the reminder that Clarence Jackson's negligence, not God's, caused his current condition.

Chapter 17

Jasper was waiting for Jane when she arrived back at the Lucky Latte. She hoped his conversations had been more profitable than hers. It's possible this was all a wild goose chase. Jax could have just gone home without feeling the need to let anyone know.

"Any luck?" asked Jane as they walked to the table in the back. That spot was turning into their usual hang-out.

"No new information about Jax. But sit down. I have some terrible news to share. Gloria Jackson is dead. Killed in a car accident last night."

Jane gasped. "Gloria dead? I just visited her at the hotel! What happened?"

"Chief Smith didn't elaborate. Frankly, I'm surprised he even mentioned it to me. It's not like I'm on the force or anything."

"He recognizes your potential to help him with the murder case. Do you think it's just a coincidence that Clarence and his ex-wife both died so close together? And both in Crooked Run?"

Jasper shook his head. "There's nothing to indicate foul play in Gloria's death. At least nothing the Chief mentioned. But I don't like coincidences, especially not where murder is concerned."

"And I can't help but wonder if Jax's disappearance somehow ties into the story as well?" said Jane.

"My brain is always trying to make patterns and connections," said Jasper.

"That's what makes you such a good detective," said Jane.

"Retired detective," said Jasper, smiling.

We need some nourishment to continue this discussion. I'll run up front and grab a menu and drinks. Do you have a coffee preference?"

"Is tea an option?"

"Of course! You're British. You need your tea!"

Jane returned with a tray filled with two mugs and a menu.

"Tea fit for the king," said Jasper as he sipped the hot Earl Grey.

"Rev. Barnard made sure I had enough tea to flood a battleship," said Jane. "I think I'll settle for coffee."

Jasper ran his eyes over the menu. "Would you like to split a spinach and portobello sandwich? I don't think I can handle a whole one. Lillie made oatmeal cookies this morning, and I'm afraid I might have overindulged."

"Her cookies are amazing!" said Jane. "Light as a feather, but filling."

"She has a knack for baking. But back to Jax — both the mayor and Chief Smith don't think there was anything unusual about Jax's behavior."

Jane nodded. "That's what I was afraid would happen. Rev. Barnard gave me a slightly different perspective, though. Were you aware Jax visited the church several times during his stay in Crooked Run?"

Jasper raised an eyebrow. "No, I was not. Did the reverend know why he was there?"

"No, Rev. Barnard is very sensitive to people and their feelings. He thought Jax needed to be left alone to meditate and pray."

"And what about the sound man, Dave?"

Jane shook her head. "No luck there either. He wasn't home, but I talked to his dad. Those two don't have an easy life staying in that dark, melancholy little house. Their place was so sad and lonely."

"That's too bad." Jasper paused as their server delivered their sandwich, a culinary masterpiece featuring thick, juicy portobello mushrooms marinated in balsamic vinegar, olive oil, and herbs and then grilled to perfection on a crusty ciabatta roll. The chef mixed a few slices of fresh avocado with the baby spinach leaves and added feta cheese crumbles on top for extra flavor.

"What a feast," said Jane, biting into the thick sandwich. "Mmmm. I taste garlic aioli!"

"This is a treat!" said Jasper, stopping to savor the rich, earthy flavor. "But back to our topic, I met a sad person today, too. Perhaps melancholy would be a better description. Young Sara, who works for Marcus. She's such a lovely lass, but her eyes looked troubled."

"She has a tough life," said Jane. "Raising a teenage boy alone can't be easy."

"No husband in the picture, then?"

"No, he left her a while back. Ran off with a hairdresser in the next town over."

"That's tragic," said Jasper, finishing the last bite of his sandwich and wiping crumbs from the tabletop. "What about Jax? Should we give up our pursuit? You must admit, the man can care for himself quite well most of the time."

"I guess you're right," said Jane. "And we need to focus on our last few choir practices."

"Right, you are!" Jasper drank the last drops of his tea and stood. "I don't think I can do justice to these chips. Want to take them with you?"

"Are you sure you don't want them?"

"No, the Fairchild sisters would be upset if I brought food into the house that someone else had made."

"Fair enough. I'll be happy to take them off your hands. You'll have to tell me how you and Emily met someday. Somehow, I feel your first attempt at telling the tale barely skimmed the surface."

"A wise and insightful observation, Rev. Jane." They walked out into the crisp autumn afternoon.

***

The church emanated a sense of tranquility and stillness as Anne sat down to play the piano. Choir rehearsal wasn't until tomorrow evening, so she had time to work out some of the dynamic transitions in the musical score. But she also needed the quiet tranquility of the old sanctuary to process her thoughts before she saw Dave again.

She hadn't been entirely honest with him in their last conversation. True, her divorce wasn't finalized. But she'd lied when she said Tom might cause problems if he found out about her and Dave. Tom had absolutely no interest in Anne or any relationships she might have. He was already in Kentucky with the singer he'd picked up at a punk rock concert. The girl was half his age and had Nashville on her mind. She hoped they were happy.

Anne was worried about Dave's 'side gig.' Caring for his dad and working for the town maintenance department took such energy. When did he have time to work at another job? But the biggest question was, what kind of job did he have? What was he doing to earn money? Did it have something to do with his visit to Denny's Digs? A visit he didn't tell her about? A visit that made him miss a date with her?

She let her fingers slide over the piano keys and picked out the melody of Ave Maria. The haunting cadence and the poignant Latin words brought tears to her eyes. What a simple, trusting woman Mary, the mother of Jesus, had been. So compliant, so willing to be the instrument of God. The melody and the story entranced her, and she didn't hear the church's back door open.

Dave stood and listened to the song's pure cadence and Anne's lovely voice as she sang the words. He wondered why the entire choir didn't drop out and let Anne sing.

The beauty of the moment made him feel more miserable. He had to get a handle on his life. He was pouring from an empty pitcher. Dave wasn't sure how long he could bear the weight of responsibility. Medical bills, rehabilitation costs, and everyday expenses were insurmountable. The piling debt left him with a sense of desperation. And now, his vulnerability had gotten him into trouble. If his dad knew…He turned and walked out of the church. He was a wretched sinner in a holy place.

Chapter 18

After she put the breakfast dishes in the sink, Jane sat down to glance at the morning paper. She started to read the front-page headlines when the doorbell rang. Who might that be at this hour?

Anne stood on the stoop, a loaf of pumpkin bread in her hand. "Jane, I'm so sorry to bother you this early. I understand you must be tired from the stress of everything that has happened the past few days."

"Come on in, Anne. I just finished eating, but I would love to have a small slice of that delicious-looking pumpkin loaf. I have enough coffee in the pot for both of us."

"Thank you, Jane. Again, I'm sorry to bother you, but I don't have anyone else to talk to. And my conscience has bothered me for a week now."

Jane looked uncomfortable. "Maybe you should talk to Rev. Barnard?"

Anne shook her head. "No, it's nothing the reverend could help with. He is the sweetest man alive, but there's no way he would understand. Jane, I'm afraid I haven't been honest with you or Chief Smith about the night Clarence Jackson died."

Jane sat down. "Go on."

"Dave and I were in the church after choir on the Wednesday Clarence was killed. You know that he and I.." she hesitated and then continued, … "that he and I have been seeing each other."

Jane nodded.

"Well, he asked me to meet him in the basement Sunday school room after choir. Said he needed to tell me something important." Anne got a tissue from her pocket. "He told me he had come up with a way to solve his money troubles and that it would be feasible for us to have a future together as soon as my divorce with Tom had come through."

"That's good news, isn't it?" Jane asked.

"I'm not sure, Jane. You see, he won't tell me what he is doing to earn money. I'm afraid if he needs to keep the information such a secret, it's something he shouldn't be doing. Plus, he seems flush with cash. I don't understand how he was broke one week and suddenly had a lot of money the next."

"I understand your concern, Anne. How can I help?"

"I'm not sure you can, Jane, but I had to tell somebody. Am I being too cautious? Should I trust him? I haven't had an excellent track record with trusting men."

"I'm not a relationship counselor. I lucked out when I met Rick. I knew he was the one almost from the start. That knowledge saved me a lot of heartache and broken relationships."

"You're so lucky, Jane." Anne looked wistful.

"I was," said Jane. "His passing left an enormous hole in my heart."

"I can't imagine." Anne wiped crumbs off the coffee table and then faced Jane. "Thank you for listening, Jane, but I need to tell you something else."

Jane nodded. "Go on."

"On the night Clarence died, I saw something I haven't told the police about. Dave and I had gone our separate ways, but I realized after I got to the car I'd left my phone in the practice room." She hesitated but took a deep breath and continued. "When I returned to get it, I saw someone enter the church's back door. I am almost sure it was Dave."

***

Emily waved a thin piece of paper in front of Vada's nose. "You're paying entirely too much money to heat this house. Where are you setting the thermostat? 80 degrees"

Vada adjusted her bifocals and looked over the fine print. "It's not any more than it usually is. Yes, we set the thermostat high, but I'm not going to walk around in six layers of clothing just to stay warm in my own house!"

"Father would turn over in his grave." Emily shook her head. "You need to leave the management of this place to me."

"Who's managing what?" Lillie entered the kitchen, leaving a mud trail from the door to the table.

"Lillie! Take off your shoes! Just look at that mess you've made!"

"I picked the last of the broccoli. I was surprised when it came back out after the snow. "I thought that cold snap would freeze it."

"Lillie! Are you not listening to a word I'm saying? Take off those shoes!" Vada pulled a small bucket from the utility closet and filled it with water.

Jasper appeared at the kitchen door. "I'm off to town, ladies. Do you need anything?"

"Yes," said Emily. "Stop by the hardware store and see if you can find a few more space heaters. You know, like the one we had in the garden shed for Jax? We are going to cut this heating bill one way or another."

"Emily, we need to discuss this first," said Vada as she pushed the mop into the soapy water and began to tackle Lillie's mud tracks. "And besides, maybe Jasper hadn't planned to go to the hardware store. You boss him around all the time, Emily. The poor man can't even have a life of his own."

"I pay him to run my errands," said Emily as she pushed aside a stack of magazines and sat on a kitchen chair. Besides, for your information, he was already going into town. To see Anne, she added with a sly smirk.

"Now, don't start a story when there is none to tell," said Jasper. "Anne and I are working on a tough piece in our competition music–the cadential extension."

"The what?" Lillie stood with her muddy shoes in her hand, staring at Jasper.

"The last two lines. It has a lot of chord changes and jumps."

"Well, you'd better figure them out. We only have a few more practices."

"Actually," said Emily, standing up and reaching for her walking stick, "I'd like to go into town with you. I need a new outfit for the choir competition."

"Me too!" said Lillie.

"Why do you need new clothes? Choir robes will cover anything you wear," said Emily.

"But we have to look nice on the way down," argued Lillie. "Isn't that right, Vada?"

"Well, you have a point, Lillie," agreed Vada. "I'd like a new outfit as well. What about dropping us off at Barkley's on your way to the church, Jasper? We'll shop while you practice."

"That sounds fine to me," said Jasper, "as long as you don't mind waiting if you finish first."

The sisters looked at each other in amusement. "No danger of that," said Vada.

***

Anne hadn't planned on walking to church, but according to the weather forecast, this was the last nice day before winter weather set in for the season. She tucked her music into her backpack, locked the front door, and began the three-block trek to the church. Pavarotti's version of Ave Maria was blaring on her phone — she'd turned up the volume to catch those last two troublesome lines. She didn't hear the car pull up beside her.

"Hey, lady!" Anne jumped and pulled out her earbuds. A man with greasy hair and an acne-covered face leered at her from an open car window.

"Can I help you?" Anne tried to stay as far away from the man as she could.

"No, but your boyfriend can."

"My boyfriend?"

"Yeah, the music man at your church. The one who looks at you with sick puppy eyes."

"Do you mean Dave? How could he possibly help you?"

He grinned. "Yeah, I thought I had the right person." His voice turned serious. "He has something that belongs to me. Something valuable. And if he doesn't return it soon, well, let's just say I wouldn't want to be in his shoes."

Before Anne could answer, the man sped away, scattering gravel and dust behind him.

***

Jane planned to spend the morning setting up her home office. Many of her reference books and sermon ideas were at her study at the church, but she wanted a spot to work from home as well. She hadn't found a desk that suited her yet, but the small folding table she'd loaned to the Fairchild sisters would work fine. They didn't need it anymore since Jax was gone. She'd call them later and ask if she could pick it up.

The familiar ringtone sounded, and Jane glanced down at her phone. Rev. Barnard.

"Good morning, reverend."

"Yes, hi, Jane." He sounded distracted. "I was wondering if you could give me some advice."

"Now that's a switch," she laughed. "I'm usually the one asking you for help."

"It's the children. I'm having trouble… I mean.., the Christmas pageant? Practice is not going well."

"I'm so sorry, Rev. Barnard, but believe me, I have my hands full at the moment. I can't tackle another duty."

"I know, I know!" he said with impatience. "I'm not asking you to take over. I simply need some help to decide which child gets what parts."

"Let me guess. Every mom wants her daughter to be Mary?"

"Why, yes." He appeared surprised that she figured out his dilemma before he even told her. "And every mother wants her son to be Joseph."

"A common problem, sir."

"But how do you choose who gets those coveted roles?" asked the puzzled parson.

"Easy," said Jane, "put the children's names in a hat and draw two."

Rev. Barnard gasped. "You mean decide the destiny of the Holy Family by fate?"

"Sure. Why not? Nobody gets to choose their family. I'm sure you don't want to get into a theological discussion, but whether you believe in predestination or free will, the family we're born into is always fate. At least from our perspective."

"You know, you're right." Rev. Barnard sounded relieved. "Thank you, Jane. You have been most helpful."

Jane smiled. If only all conundrums could be solved by slips of paper in a hat.

The clock struck 11 a.m. She'd call the Fairchild sisters and set a time to go over and pick up the table. They had made it clear that she was welcome anytime, but she wasn't comfortable dropping in unannounced.

She dialed their landline number. After seven rings, she got the answering machine. The sisters had a habit of not answering the phone when they were busy with a project, so she punched in Vada's mobile number. Vada answered after two rings.

"Jane, how nice to hear your voice! I trust all is well."

"Hello, Vada. Yes, all is well. Would it be okay to stop by your house in about a quarter of an hour? I need to pick up my table—the one I let Jax borrow."

"Yes, yes, of course! Unfortunately, we are trying on clothes at Barkley's, but the garden shed is open. Go in and pick up your table."

"Thank you, Vada. I'll run over in a few minutes."

"I'm sorry we're not at home. I would love to visit with you."

"I'll come back again soon," promised Jane.

The clouds gathered as she drove down Main Street, past the town buildings and offices. She hoped the weather wouldn't turn bad again. These last few days of practice were crucial to their performance.

Jane caught sight of Jasper's car as she passed the church. She was tempted to stop in for a quick visit but decided not to interrupt. He and Anne had some serious work to do.

She parked in the Fairchild driveway and stopped to admire the stately old structure. It was a perfect example of a Victorian country house. Ahead, Jane saw a flock of migrating geese. What a peaceful place, what a tranquil afternoon.

As promised, the door to the garden shed was unlocked. Jane's table stood stark and bare in the middle of the room. As she turned the table to the side to collapse the legs, something fell to the floor. A red folder.

Curious, she picked it up. Scrawled on the front of the folder was the name "Jax." Now, even more interested, she opened it. Inside were newspaper clippings, articles, photographs, and hand-scribbled notes. Someone must have taped the folder to the bottom of the table.

Should she take the papers to the police? Chief Smith had already marked Jax off his suspect list. Still… She tucked the folder under her arm and loaded the table into the back of her truck.

***

The car had followed Dave since he'd left the town office. He'd stopped for gas, and the black Cadillac pulled into a music store across the street. Now, back on the road, the vehicle appeared again in his rearview mirror. He knew it would stop at his house. He hoped his dad wasn't sitting near the window.

Dave signaled to turn into his driveway. The Cadillac signaled as well.

"You didn't show up for our last meeting," said the man as Dave got out of his car. "You have something that belongs to me."

Dave stuffed his hands deeper into his pockets but said nothing.

The man moved closer. Smiley Parsons didn't like being stood up. He didn't get this far to be pushed around by one wimpy man. The boss told him to help, and he did. Now, the dude didn't want to pay up. That's not how it worked. He was reluctant to call the boss. The boss didn't like to be bothered. He paid Smiley well to handle the details, and handle them he would.

"I will give you one chance." He held an oil-stained finger in Dave's face. "One. If you want your girlfriend to stay alive and well, you won't fail."

"Anne?" Dave forgot about keeping the noise from his dad. "You leave Anne out of this! She has nothing to do with it."

The man leered. "I'm afraid, my friend, it's too late to leave her out."

Dave leaped at the man and pushed him against the car. "What have you done with Anne?" he snarled. "Where is she?"

Smiley jerked away from Dave's grip. "Look, man, I'm asking the questions here. You give me a satisfactory answer, and we'll talk. Your girlfriend is fine. We had a pleasant conversation. That's all."

Dave wanted to wipe the leer off the man's face. He wanted to punch him until he could no longer stand. But he knew that would be a foolish move. Dave dropped his head. "I'll have it by the weekend. I promise."

Chapter 19

Anne was out of breath when she reached the church. She sat on the step for a moment to regain her composure before meeting with Jasper. How could she think about singing when a menacing ruffian was after Dave? The encounter with the creep on the street scared her, but the reason he targeted her frightened her more. She almost convinced herself that Dave was involved with drugs. Why else would it be so secretive? She was lost in thought and didn't notice when Jasper sat beside her.

"Anne, are you OK?."

She looked up in surprise. "Oh, hi, Jasper. I didn't know you were here."

"Is everything OK?" he repeated. "You look as though you've seen a ghost."

Anne glanced out over the parking lot to the street beyond. She thought she glimpsed the black Cadillac turning onto Myrtle Street–Dave's place. "A demon is more like it," she said.

***

"That green pantsuit makes you look like a pea pod," said Emily as Lillie displayed her purchase.

Lillie scowled. "And that purple tunic you bought just turned you into a bunch of grapes!"

The sisters gathered their shopping bags and walked to the department store's door as Jasper pulled up.

"That man has an impeccable sense of timing," said Vada, motioning for the others to follow.

"He's quite capable," said Emily, speaking like a proud parent. "I wonder why some female hasn't snatched him up by now. He's handsome, kind, and eligible."

"Is he, though?" asked Lillie thoughtfully. "Something tells me he might have left someone behind in England."

"Oh, so now you're psychic," said Emily.

Lillie shook her head. "Not psychic. Only observant. He has an air of sadness about him sometimes. A faraway look."

"I've known him for two years," said Emily, "and I've never seen him with a woman. He hasn't even talked about one."

"Maybe not," said Lillie, "but I think he has a long, sad, romantic tale to tell. I'll get it out of him sometime."

"Hello, ladies!" Jasper expertly took all three bags and stored them in the trunk as the sisters settled into the car. "How was your shopping? Did you find some bargains?"

"I think we did very well," said Vada. "But I'm pooped! I'll take a nap when we get home. How did practice go, Jasper?"

"I believe we've sorted through most of the tricky parts." Jasper wished he could solve Anne's tangled dilemma as easily as they'd worked out the music.

**

Jane took the long way back to her house. The day was beautiful, even though the wind had picked up and the clouds were turning darker. The red folder piqued her curiosity, but she waited until after dinner to look through it. She felt tempted to call Jasper to come over and review the information with her. But what if it turned out to be nothing? Just random clippings of an aging man? No, she'd look at it first, and then, if she deemed it important enough, she'd call Jasper.

After she washed and put away the dinner dishes, Jane sat at her kitchen table and spread out the folder's contents.

Her initial impression was that they were a random stack of news clippings and held meaning only for the person who collected them. But after a while, she noticed a pattern in the stories. The clippings at the top were all about a drug bust during the late 1970s. She pieced the stories together chronologically before she tried to make sense of it. It started in December 1978 when three young men were involved in an altercation with several drug dealers in Oakland, California. The youths faced trial after one of the drug dealers was shot and killed. They sentenced two of the suspected shooters to ten years in prison, while the third man walked away without charges.

These stories meant something to Jax, but what? Presumably, he knew the people involved. Was Jax a dealer? She was about to return the clippings to the folder when a picture caught her eye. The article was thin and yellow with age. However, as she held the photo to the light, she was sure she recognized two of the faces. She took out her phone and snapped a picture, enlarging the photo with her fingers. She struggled to distinguish the words in the faded caption, but the names were there: Daniel "Jax" Porter, Clarence Jackson, and Sydney Lincoln.

Jane's heart skipped a beat. Jax and Clarence! A connection did exist, after all! She needed to tell someone. Chief Smith would accuse her of manufacturing stories; he'd dismissed all her earlier efforts. She would call Jasper.

***

Marcus was not in the office that afternoon, and Sara wanted to leave early. She needed a break. The past few weeks had been stressful. The water main break, the choir competition, Brayden's practice schedule, and … that other thing. She wished she weren't so desperate for money. The lack of funds caused people to do things they would never otherwise consider. She had to find a way out.

The hands on the wall clock moved in slow motion—thirty-five more minutes. The front door clicked. Most likely Marcus. So much for her plan for an early escape.

"Oh, good, Sara, you're still here. Cinda is coming back Sunday afternoon, so my days as a single man about town are dwindling. And I imagine Lady Jane will have us practicing the rest of the weekend. I'll be glad when that competition is over. So, what about dinner tonight?"

Sara looked down at her desk to prevent him from seeing her face. "I was hoping to have a quiet dinner with Brayden this evening. He's struggling with his honors English class, and I wanted to encourage him and give him some pointers with his essay."

Marcus snorted. "You coddle that boy too much. How's the kid ever supposed to make it on his own if you continue to bail him out? A man needs to learn to stand on his own two feet."

"He's only sixteen," she whispered. "He has a way to go before he becomes a man."

"Train 'em right from the start. That's what I always say. However, I am glad that Cinda never wanted children. What do you say? Shall I pick you up at seven? That will give you plenty of time to help your boy with his homework."

Sara sighed, and Marcus continued. "I hear senior pictures are expensive this year. And what about that senior trip? Somebody said they're planning to go to Europe next summer. How will you be able to foot the bill for that?"

Sara lowered her head so Marcus would not see the tears in her eyes.

"Seven will be fine," she said.

***

Anne wasn't afraid to walk back home. She was, however, conscious of every vehicle that passed. She was surprised to see Dave's car in her driveway.

"Hey! I didn't expect to see you here. What's up?"

"Anne, we need to talk. Let's take a drive over to Waypoint. I owe you a dinner."

Anne hesitated. Part of her wanted to listen to what Dave had to say, and part of her didn't trust him.

"Please, Anne?"

"Dave, I am so confused. I want to trust you. I truly do. So tell me your story. But you have to promise to be upfront with me. No more secrets."

"No more secrets."

They drove in silence for a while.

"Dave, tell me. What is this all about?"

Dave sighed. "Since Dad's accident, we have been living on a shoestring budget. The insurance promised to pay a lot more than came through. I have maxed out all our credit cards and still don't have enough to make ends meet."

"Dave, I did not know. You mentioned that money is tight, but I didn't know you were hurting so much. The other day you were carrying around a lot of cash. Why didn't you reach out? I'm sure folks in the church would be happy to help."

"Anne, you don't understand. We owe thousands and thousands of dollars. The church wouldn't be able to help that much."

"But we have friends outside the church who would help. Dave, you don't have to do this alone!"

"They can't help now, Anne. I was sure I'd found an easy way to earn extra money. Lots of money. Yet, I should know by now if something appears too good to be true, it almost always is."

"Dave, what did you do?" Anne had a profound sense of dread.

"I got in with the wrong crowd. At first, it didn't seem like it. Some respectable people were involved. Or at least I assumed they were respectable. Turns out I was mistaken. Anne, I'm in over my head. I can't escape."

Anne hesitated. "These people you're involved with… I assume the guy who threatened me on my way to church is one of the 'wrong crowd'?"

Dave looked miserable. "Yes, I owe them money, too."

"There has to be a way out of this," said Anne. "We can tell the authorities."

"You don't understand. Some powerful people are part of the group.

Some so-called " good guys" are the "bad guys."

"What do you mean?"

"I'm not at liberty to say who, but let's just say there are people involved who we don't want to double cross. Trust me, I will find a way out of this, but I want you to be safe while I work it out."

"Dave, I can take care of myself. You have enough on your mind. What about your dad? Does he know about this?"

Dave shook his head. "He's miserable enough without knowing his son is a loser."

"I need to ask you something. Dave, did you go back into the church after practice on the night Clarence was killed? Did you murder Clarence?"

Dave pulled into the La Belle Italian Restaurant parking lot and turned off the motor. "Yes. I went back into the church. And no. I did not kill Clarence."

Anne sighed with relief. "But why did you go back inside?"

Dave hung his head. "Edith hadn't deposited Sunday's offering yet. I..."

"You stole money from the church?" Anne gasped.

"I was going to borrow it. I planned to give it back. Somehow. Anne, you saw that man. Any one of them would kill me as quickly as they would smash a bug."

"And you gave them the stolen money?"

Dave looked miserable. "I carried it in my car for a few days, but I couldn't do it. I took the money back to the church. And now, I have a dangerous thug on my tail demanding repayment, and I have nothing."

"I feel like there's an integral part to this story that you aren't telling me. How did you get involved in this mess? Dave, these are not the kinds of people you normally hang out with."

"I can't tell you, Anne," he said. "I know all of this will come crashing down soon, but until it does, I can't talk about it."

"Take me home, Dave. We can't be friends until you're willing to be honest with me."

Chapter 20

Jane had a restless night. Visions of drug wars, shootings, and Jax filled her dreams. She woke early and made a cup of black coffee. She didn't want to call Jasper at five a.m. Opening the red folder, she flipped through the articles. The faded print was sometimes challenging to read, but bit by bit, Jane was piecing together a story. She ran a quick search on Daniel Porter and Clarence Jackson of Oakland, California. Sydney Lincoln seemed to have fared better than the other two. He might have been an innocent bystander. As far as she could tell, he didn't serve any jail time.

Daniel Porter and Sydney Lincoln disappeared from any online sources after the drug incident. Clarence Jackson, however, had a strong Internet presence. He turned his life around after that initial wrong turn. They released him after three years for exemplary behavior. The next listing she found showed Clarence in his mid-twenties as a student at the University of California. She found later pictures of him at Julliard performing in an orchestral production. So, his stories were confirmed. The ones he shared, that is.

Had Jax followed Clarence to the Shenandoah Valley? Why, after all these years, would he want to connect with his old friend? And why didn't he say anything about knowing Clarence? Why didn't Clarence say anything about him? And who was Sydney Lincoln?

Jane called the Fairchild house shortly after nine, hoping to talk to Jasper.

"Jane, what a pleasant surprise," said Vada. "Emily got the idea of cleaning out all the other bedrooms in this house today. Not that she will lift a finger to help. Being a 'supervisor' is more her style, she says. She wants to open up the boarding house again."

"She's quite ambitious." Jane tried to keep the conversation short without seeming rude.

"That's our Emily, always planning other people's lives for them."

"And their deaths!" Jane heard Lillie shouting in the background.

Jane laughed. "Is Jasper at home?" She hadn't meant to be so direct, but her mind was stuck on the red folder and its contents.

"Yes, he is. Hold on a moment while I call him."

***

Jasper was at Jane's house in less than the ten minutes he'd promised her.

"I hope I didn't take you away from the big cleaning project." Jane handed him a mug of coffee and a plate of oatmeal cookies.

"I was quite relieved to come over here. Miss Emily was going to have me climb onto the turret and wash the upper windows." Jasper shuddered. "I've always struggled with the fear of heights. Now, what can I do for you?"

Jane handed him the folder and explained where it came from. "Why don't you sit in the living room near the bay window? There's more light there. Reading through the stories might take you a while. Some of those articles have faded and are difficult to make out."

Jasper settled in the recliner near the window and examined the folder's contents. Jane was silent as he read. Occasionally, he would whistle under his breath, and once in a while, he held an article close to the window for more light. Finally, he closed the folder and sighed. "I'm more confused now than I was earlier. I wish we had seen this before Jax disappeared."

"Me too," said Jane. "He might have been able to answer many of our questions."

"Wonder who this Sydney Lincoln is," said Jasper. "He seems to have disappeared after the first article."

"No clue. I searched the name online and found half a dozen people by that name. None of them were the right age. I guess he'd be around Jax's age by now."

"As far as I can tell, these articles do nothing but make a positive connection between Jax and Clarence. Still, that's pretty big."

"Yes," said Jane. "As pompous as Clarence was, I can understand why he might not want to associate with a man like Jax. He may have believed that the relationship would damage his reputation."

"I don't like the idea, but we have to give this information to Chief Smith. It might shed some light on Clarence's past. It may also give some clues about the murder. This is too big for us. Do you want me to run this folder over to the police station?"

"I'll make copies of the file first," said Jane. "And after that, I'll take them by Smith's office. And please, keep me in the loop if you find out anything about Jax."

"Will do. And you do the same."

***

The police station appeared deserted, except for a single cruiser. Jane hoped Brad Harris would be on duty. She didn't want to talk to Chief Smith. But luck was not on her side. Deputy Harris was leaving as she arrived.

"Off to keep Crooked Run safe, Deputy Harris?" Jane asked as they passed on the steps.

"Off to pick up groceries for Ms. Thomas," he grinned. "She has a nasty case of gout, and she says she can't walk."

"You're a good man, Deputy."

Jane walked past the glass doors to the Town Office and headed straight to the Police Station. Chief Smith was sitting at his desk, scrolling through some black-and-white photos on his computer. He looked up as Jane entered.

"Rev. Cartwright. What brings you by this early in the morning?"

"I have something I need to give you," said Jane.

Chief Smith pulled out a chair and motioned for her to sit.

Jane began, "Yesterday afternoon, I picked up a table from the Fairchild's garden shed."

"You mean the place where that strange man, Jax, was hiding?"

Jane felt a flash of anger but kept her voice steady. "Yes, the Fairchild sisters were kind enough to allow Jax to stay in their garden shed during that early snowstorm. The mayor was perfectly fine with leaving him outside to freeze," she added.

"You understand that was a very dangerous thing you did." Smith narrowed his eyes and looked at Jane.

"I've already been over this with the mayor. You and the Crooked Run police cleared Jax of any wrongdoing. I was in the building when you released him from being a suspect in Clarence's murder."

"Just happened to be there, did you?" Smith narrowed his eyes.

"Yes, I was pleading with the mayor to find a place for the poor man to stay."

Smith stood up and walked toward the window. "We don't have enough money in our town budget to build homeless shelters. People should find these things out before they come here.

"Chief Smith, the world is full of 'shoulds' and 'musts.' You can speculate all day about how to create a perfect society. The reality is that there are always going to be unhoused people. Ignoring the situation or passing responsibility on to someone else doesn't address the actual issue."

"So your solution was to send a stranger to live with three helpless old ladies?"

"You know quite well they are not helpless old ladies. And they have a Scotland Yard detective staying with them."

"Retired Scotland Yard," said Smith.

"Chief Smith, do you want to argue semantics, or can I give you the information I found?"

Chief Smith grunted. "Go on. What do you have for me?"

Jane handed him the folder. "As I said earlier when I picked up my table from the Fairchild's garden shed, this folder fell out from under it. You might find some items of interest in it."

"What's this? Looks like a bunch of old newspaper clippings." Smith seemed to lose interest as he flipped through the folder.

"Read them," said Jane. "Or read one."

Smith turned on a desk lamp and put on his glasses. He blew a soft whistle when he came to the article with the picture. "That homeless man had a connection with Clarence Jackson? Now that's a surprise."

"It surprised me, too," Jane said.

"What surprised you?" The door opened, and the mayor of Crooked Run came into the office.

"Working on a Saturday. Now, that's what I call dedication." He patted Smith on the back. "What are you reading?"

Smith handed the article to Marcus.

"What's this? Some newspaper archive?" Marcus sat down and read. Jane watched his face change from white to red. He stood up and slammed the newspaper clippings on the table. "That does it! We've got to find that man. I warned you not to let him go. I told you he was guilty. And what do you do? You conduct one little DNA test and release him."

"Calm down, mayor. You agreed we had no evidence to hold Jax."

"Something always bothered me about that man. And now we uncover all of this." he pointed to the folder. "Smith, you go find that man, and you find him quickly, or I'll have your badge."

Chief Smith's eyes widened. "Mayor, I'm on it. I'll call Harris back in, and we'll send out an APB. Don't worry. We'll have him back in custody in no time."

Marcus looked doubtful. "See to it." He turned to Jane. "What do you have to do with this?"

"I found that folder taped to the bottom of a table I loaned Jax when he stayed with the Fairchild sisters."

Marcus looked disgusted. "I still can't believe you let him stay there."

Jane was in no mood to continue to defend her actions in helping to find shelter for Jax.

"Jane," he continued in a low voice, "Does anybody else know about this new information?"

"I shared it with Jasper."

"Oh, so he's more than your music partner? Well, make sure you don't say anything to anyone else. I don't want to jeopardize this investigation. We need to bring that killer to justice."

***

"Jane, dear, it's Bethel. Time's getting close!" Bethel's singsong voice made Jane cringe. The last person she wanted to talk to was her rival for the choir competition. "How is that dishy British man coming along?"

"What do you mean?" asked Jane.

"I mean, does he have a voice to match his looks?" Bethel giggled.

Jane had just left the police office and was in no mood for idle chatter. She was definitely not in the mood to talk to Bethel.

"I have reservations on the Speeddog charter bus line. The bus is big enough for both of our choirs. Would you like me to book seats for your group, too?"

Marcus was supposed to make travel arrangements, but he'd only confirmed their hotel rooms so far. Jane had no desire to spend six hours trapped on a bus with Bethel and her choir, but economically speaking, that might be the best thing to do.

"I'll run it past my choir. I'll call you after practice."

"Alright. Sounds good! Tootles!"

Chapter 21

Chief Smith sat staring at the results of the traffic crash investigation. Gloria Jackson had not been drinking. They had not found a trace of alcohol in her bloodstream. Someone had cut the brake lines on her car. He had another murder on his hands.

***

Jane was poring over the copies she'd made of the newspaper clippings in the red folder when her doorbell rang. For an instant, she considered snatching up the papers and hiding them, but she answered the door instead.

It was Jax.

Jane wasn't sure whether to invite him inside or talk to him on the porch. She still wasn't convinced he was a killer, but she approached the situation cautiously.

"May I come in, ma'am?" said Jax, bowing. "I don't mean to inconvenience you, but I need to talk to you about some things."

Jane eased aside and allowed the man to enter. "Where have you been, Jax? We have all been so worried about you."

Jax shook his head, tight-lipped.

"I made a pot of coffee, and I'll see if I have some muffins left from breakfast this morning." Jane led him into the kitchen. She immediately realized her mistake when he saw the copies of the newspaper articles lying all across the table.

"My folder. You found my folder." Jax's eyes filled with tears.

"Yes." Jane stacked the papers and moved them to the side. "Do you want to tell me about the articles?"

Jax bowed his head. "I would rather leave all of this in the past. In the old days, where it belongs. But someone has unearthed the dragon, and we must extinguish its fire. Even now, someone is trying to kill me."

Jane gasped. "What do you mean, Jax? Did someone threaten you? Are you in danger?"

"We are all in danger." Jax bowed his head.

Jane felt her heart race. Had someone followed Jax here? Should she call the police? She said slowly, "Jax, you must tell me what's happening. If we're in danger, I need to call Chief Smith."

Jax grew agitated. "No! No! You cannot call the police. I won't let them lock me up. This time, they won't give me food and take care of me. This time, they will send me to the big prison."

"Calm down, Jax. I won't call Chief Smith yet. Can you sit down at the table and tell me your story?"

Jax sat by the window, took off his hat, and sipped coffee. He nodded to himself as though coming to a decision. "Many years ago, I was part of a group that was not good. There were people in it who didn't care about other people. All they cared about was getting money. A lot of money. You can tell from the clippings that I spent some time in jail."

"And Clarence, too. He spent time in jail as well." Jane didn't bother to put this information in question form.

"Yes. Clarence too. It was Clarence who called me here."

Jane was terrified. What if Jax did murder Clarence? Her phone was in her pocket. Should she call 911?

"Did you.." she hesitated, "did you send Clarence a threatening note? Did you kill Clarence?"

"No, ma'am. I did not kill Clarence." Jax twisted his battered hat in his hands. "I came here to help him. The entire mission was flawed. Nothing went as planned."

"What was your plan, Jax? Let me get you some more coffee, and you can sit back and tell me the complete story."

She filled Jax's cup again and put two more muffins on a plate. "Did you have breakfast? Would you like some eggs and bacon?"

"The coffee and muffins are good," he said, taking a long drink. He picked up the newspaper clipping with the photo at the bottom of the page. "We were young. I didn't expect this wrong turn to follow us throughout our lives. He should have let go of it. I shouldn't have listened to him."

"Jax, can you try to start at the beginning of the story? You need to understand that I don't know what happened to you in the past. The story is clear in your mind, but it isn't in mine."

"I understand," said Jax. "It's hard for me. My ideas don't run in a line.

They go in and out of time."

"Were you friends with Clarence when you were young?" Jane asked, trying to help Jax organize his thoughts so that he could tell his story.

"We were friends for a long time, from the early days. We were seventeen when the bad guys came to our neighborhood. They had drugs they were selling to the students in our high school."

"You and Clarence sold drugs?"

"We got involved, yes. For a while, we made money. A lot of money. But then, the trouble came."

Jane poured more coffee into Jax's empty cup.

"Another group of people moved into our neighborhood. A group of men who were older and tougher than our group. They told us we had to work for them or stop our selling operation altogether. Well, by this time, we were making a lot of money, and we didn't like the looks of the new people."

Jane thought she heard a car pull up outside, but a casual glance out of the window revealed no one. It must have passed on down the road.

"One day, there was a fight. A territory fight. Somebody killed one of the bad guys. With my gun. The police arrested us and sent us to jail. The police said they wanted to make an example of Clarence and me. Guess he assumed that by throwing the book at us, other kids would hesitate before getting involved in drugs. We each got ten years."

"What about the third boy in the photo? Sydney Lincoln. Didn't he go to jail as well?"

Jax sighed. "That's the trouble. The mess today would not have happened if he had been in jail with us."

"He escaped?"

"No, he didn't go. His dad had a lot of money and had powerful contacts. Sydney stayed in jail overnight, and then they let him go. Said he learned his lesson. I'm not sure why it took me ten years when he got out in twenty-four hours. No, ma'am, it never made sense to me."

Jax looked out the window into the forest, his gaze thoughtful.

"I'm still confused, Jax. I don't see the connection between what happened in the past and Clarence's death. And this third boy? How does he fit in?"

Jax sighed. "A few days ago, someone gave me money to leave Crooked Run. Enough money for me to go back home. For a while, I agreed I should leave this place. My mission here did not work out. I got a ride with a nice trucker who took me as far as Tennessee. But I was restless. I had left everything in a mess. So I thanked him and started walking back here. Back to Crooked Run. Back to finish what I started."

A chill ran down Jane's spine. "What you started?"

Jax seemed irritated. She was asking too many questions. She should understand his story by now.

"Clarence is dead, so it's my mission to carry out justice. But I can't do it like Clarence wanted to. That was wrong. Profiting from someone else's wickedness."

Jane tried to keep calm. She understood he was trying his best to explain his story.

"Who was the third man? This Sydney Lincoln?"

Before Jax could answer, a voice behind her said, "What an excellent question."

***

Sara scraped the food from her plate and into the trash can. She wasn't hungry. Brayden had woofed down his lunch and had gone off to practice music at his friend's house. She looked at the pile of envelopes on the counter. Bills she could not pay. The arrangement she had with Marcus had to end. She reached a point where she couldn't continue playing his game. It was a complete violation of her moral code.

The relationship wasn't physical. She might have been able to rationalize that. But the more she became involved in 'side business,' the more she questioned the ethics of the situation. Now, she was sure what he was doing was against the law.

***

"My throat is killing me," said Lillie as she stirred a mixture of honey and lemon tea. "We have three days until the concert, and it feels like someone has set my entire neck on fire. Edith will have to lead the alto section if I don't feel better soon. And we might as well give up any hope of a blue ribbon if that happens."

"Add a little ginger to that mix, and you'll be right as rain by this evening." Emily came into the kitchen carrying a stack of spiral notebooks. "And if worse comes to worse, I can take your place. My voice was quite the rage in high school." She plopped the notebooks on the table. "Plans," she said. "I found Father's original notes for this hotel. He has some amazing ideas. We'd do well to scrap everything we've created so far and go with his blueprint."

"Don't be daft, Emily," said Vada. "These plans might have worked when he first used them eighty years ago. I, for one, don't want to be tied down making three meals a day. And besides, people these days have such strange dietary requirements–keto, vegan, gluten-free, vegetarian–how would it be possible to stock a pantry to include these options? Not to mention allergies–peanuts, dairy, seafood. We would face lawsuits within the first three days of operations."

"We'd need to write some disclaimers up front: if you have food allergies or specific dietary needs, you'll need to provide your own meals."

"I'm sure our place would be overloaded with guests," Vada said. Her tone dripped with sarcasm.

"Leave the planning to me," said Emily. "I am the eldest and the wisest."

"And the one who poisoned a vicar," added Lillie. "Just wait till that word gets out. I'm sure people will clamor to stay in the boarding house where the cook poisoned a man."

"A mistake I won't make again," said Emily. "Once burned, twice shy."

"You keep dreaming, sister. In the meantime, if my throat isn't better by the morning, I'm afraid I will have to call Jane and tell her she might need to find another alto."

Chapter 22

Jane turned around. Standing at her door was the mayor of Crooked Run. "Marcus, I didn't hear you come in."

He pushed past her into the house. "That was my plan," he said, pulling out a kitchen chair without being offered a seat. "You should lock your doors. You don't know the kinds of riff-raff that roam around." He glared at Jax. "Why did you come back? Don't you think you did enough damage the first time you were here? I thought we had made a deal to keep you away for good."

Jane stood to face the men. "It's time you both stop beating around the bush and tell me what's going on."

Marcus raised an eyebrow. "Are you sure you want to find out, Jane? I'm afraid the information will mean I need to silence you."

"What do you mean?"

Jax had stood as well and backed away from the table.

"Oh, no, you don't," said Marcus, moving toward him. "You know too much. I can't let you go. You had your chance to escape, but here you are."

"Sit back down. I will tell you the whole sordid story. But before we delve into the past, let me give you a glimpse of your future. Sadly, Chief Smith will find a murder-suicide situation when he stops by your house. Or maybe your pal, the Scotland Yard Bobby, will be the one to find you. Crooked Run Chronicle headlines will read: 'Crooked Run's assistant pastor done in by a drifter–a homeless man she had tried to befriend.' A tragedy, but life is not always fair."

Jane carefully pulled the phone from her pocket, but Marcus snatched it from her hand. "Oh no, Jane. That would be far too easy. Were you going to call your British buddy? Or Chief Smith? I'm sorry, but that won't work." He pulled a gun from his pocket. "This." He patted the revolver, "will make sure that you move as I wish and say the words I want you to say."

Jane put both hands on the table and motioned for Jax to do the same.

Marcus put the gun back into his pocket. "Now," he said, "there is some truth in the fact criminals enjoy sharing their stories with their victims. We want a few people to recognize our cleverness. Too bad these folks are not around long enough to spread our notoriety." He gave Jane a meaningful glance. "But it is nice to tell our tales once in a while. Alas, poor Clarence was already familiar with my story, so it would have been pointless for me to waste time talking to him. His end was sure and swift."

"You killed Clarence." Jane needed to make sure he continued talking - extending his story for as long as possible. That was her only hope for not becoming Marcus's next victim. Maybe, just maybe, someone would come to visit. Was it too much to hope that Jasper would stop by?

"Once upon a time," began Marcus, "there was a boy named Sydney Lincoln. When he was young, his family moved from Crooked Run to Southern California. This boy belonged to a wealthy family. His father was a prominent lawyer, and his mother was a renowned doctor."

"You're Sydney Lincoln?" Jane asked, surprised, but the story was making sense.

"In the flesh," grinned Marcus. "Or at least I was. But back to my story. This boy and his friends got involved in a little drug drama right after high school. A rival dealer got a little peeved that the kid and his two friends were making money. Especially since they were selling in an exclusive area—or so the dealer assumed. This dealer challenged the boys to a fight. The winner got the selling rights."

Jax groaned, and Marcus glared at him. "What's the matter? Can't bear to hear the details of your past? Don't want Rev. Jane to know what a scoundrel you were?"

Jax dropped his head to his chest.

"Well, the boy and his friends—that would be Clarence, Jax, and me— got a jump on the fight. We visited the enemy's hangout the evening before. They had no clue what hit them! One of their guys got shot and killed."

"You shot him in the back," said Jax, his silence broken.

"Details, details." Marcus twirled the gun like a baton.

"And Clarence and I ended up in jail for your crime."

"Wrong place, wrong time," said Marcus. "Fortunately, this is one situation my parents came through for me. They knew the judge and his weakness for money. I got off with a wrist slap."

Jax started to move toward Marcus, and Marcus pulled out the gun again. "Watch it, buddy. No sudden moves. I'm giving you the luxury of a few minutes more to live. Don't jeopardize it."

Jax sat back down.

"After that incident, I decided it might be good for me to turn over a new leaf. Move across the country. Start a new life. Create a new identity. And so I moved back east to Virginia, and Marcus was born."

Jane shook her head in disbelief.

"You must admit my change was a success," said Marcus with pride. "For over forty years, I have lived an exemplary life. My neighbors respect me, town officials trust me, and I sing in the church choir. A testament to my ingenuity."

"God will judge you," said Jax. "The wicked shall be turned into hell."

"Why did you and Clarence assume you could outsmart me?" asked Marcus, ignoring Jax's warning. "Why did you listen to him? I was going to let him live here peacefully and anonymously until he started that old black-mail trick. $5000, and he'd keep quiet. Then $10,000, and he wouldn't say a word. I soon realized that his demands wouldn't end. He'd hound me till the day I died. Or, as fate would have it, the day he died." Marcus grinned. "What'd he offer you, Jax? A share in the profit if you'd join his cause?"

Jax shook his head. "I was seeking justice. Nothing more. Clarence told me I owed that to him. To help keep you in check before you hurt someone else. But I was too late, wasn't I?"

"What do you mean?"

"You never stopped dealing, did you?"

Marcus laughed. "My side business has nothing to do with you. But since you won't be around to ruin my reputation, I will give you the satisfaction of telling you that you're correct. I have a business network that covers much of the Valley."

"Be sure your sin will find you out." Jax's gaze didn't waver.

"Hey, I tried some of your religious quotes on Clarence. I considered it only fair to give him a little heads-up before he met his maker. 'Prepare to meet thy God.' Pretty clever, no? I knew he'd blame you. Quoting the Good Book is your thing, not mine."

"Were you to blame for the speaker that nearly crushed Clarence?"

"Oh, that." Marcus waved his hand across his face as though the incident were a minor detail. "I didn't expect it to hit him—although it was possible. It didn't take much to loosen the bolts on the speaker's chain. I couldn't predict when it would fall, so I didn't think it would work. Still," he rubbed his hands together, "sometimes we can get lucky. Imagine, if the speaker had done its job, this story would have a different ending."

"But you could have killed anyone—a child might have walked under

144

the speaker as it fell. You were willing to risk innocent lives to have your revenge?"

"Collateral damage," said Marcus. "Nobody ever said life was fair. Just ask poor Gloria Jackson."

"What do you mean?" asked Jane. "She died in a car accident. Did you…"

"You can't trust the brakes on those Teslas. First, it was the suspension and steering columns." Marcus smirked.

"You tampered with the brakes?"

"A right tool and two minutes can make a nice little slice in the brake lines."

Jax put his head in his hands and wept. Jane moved to comfort him, but Marcus waved the gun in her direction. "Stand still, Jane. Don't make me shoot you before I'm ready."

Jane moved away from Jax. "But why did you kill Gloria?"

"Jane, Jane! I'm disappointed with you. Surely, you're clever enough to know that Gloria also knew Sydney Lincoln. It took her less than a minute to connect me with that long-ago persona. She sealed her fate the minute the light of recognition dawned in her eyes."

"So what are your plans now?" said Jane, realizing that Marcus's story was coming to a close.

"My plans? Why, keep on living as a model citizen of Crooked Run. After I alert the police about the tragic murder-suicide, they might give me a medal or something. No one will doubt, Jax, that you killed Clarence and Jane," Marcus smirked. "Sure, the choir will miss the competition this year, but who knows, I might lead them to a win next year."

Without warning, Jax jumped from the table and put his hands around Marcus's throat. "You will not get away this time," said Jax, fumbling for Marcus's gun. He was too late. Jane heard the shot at the same time her doorbell rang.

***

Jasper did not want to stress Jane, but all three Fairchild sisters now had the same worrisome throat ailment. He'd made gallons of lemon tea spiced with ginger and cloves, but they seemed to get worse; Jane would lose two of her ten singers only days before the contest unless a minor miracle happened.

He'd tried Jane's cell phone, but it went straight to voicemail. He was glad when Lillie sent him to the store for chicken soup. That would allow him to drop in on Jane and tell her the unfortunate news. As he neared the house, the sound of raised voices startled him. He sensed something was amiss and headed toward the window for a better view. He stepped back in

145

horror as he saw the mayor of Crooked Run holding a gun over a slumped body. What had happened? Had someone tried to attack Jane? Was Marcus the hero or the villain?

Jasper's hands shook as he dialed 911. Years of experience had taught him that a surprise attack, while risky, might be his best bet at stopping the stand-off. He rang the doorbell and then hurried back to the window. Jasper had a split second to react. Saying a prayer to St. Michael, the patron saint of police officers, he grabbed a brick from the front flower bed and threw it through the largest pane.

The sudden sound of shattering glass caught Marcus off guard. His momentary distraction allowed Jasper to open the window, enter the room, and swiftly pull Jane behind him. Jax lay on the floor, white and still.

"Well, if it isn't the British Bobby," snarled Marcus, his gun pointed at Jasper. "You've complicated my little plan but have not rendered it useless. Just changed it to a suicide and a double homicide. The tragedies will be close enough that authorities won't suspect that the suicide happened before the homicides."

The wail of a siren pierced the air. Jasper had hoped they would run a muted call to give him a few more minutes to plan and to keep Marcus distracted, but luck wasn't on his side.

"Can we talk about this rationally?" asked Jasper.

"Rationally?" Marcus's voice held a hint of hysteria. "We're beyond reason. He waved the gun."

"Drop it, Marcus. It's over." Chief Smith's voice came through the broken window glass. "You have one chance to come out."

Marcus fired.

***

Jane had a strong aversion to hospitals. Their sterile whiteness brought back too many memories of Rick's last hours: the beeping monitors, the muted footsteps, and the dull silver medicine carts.

Thank God Jasper's wound had been superficial. The bullet grazed his shoulder. He'd lost a bit of blood, so they were keeping him for observation. Jax was in critical condition.

She was grateful that Sara was there to sit with her.

"I brought you some hot chocolate and a chicken salad sandwich." Sara's voice was quiet as she joined Jane on the small waiting room sofa.

"Thank you so much for coming," said Jane. "I hope Brayden is okay at home alone."

"Oh, he's over at Chris's house. He doesn't spend a lot of time with his dad, but once in a while, he asks to go over. Chris bought him a new set of guitar strings."

"I'm so worried about Jax. He lost a lot of blood. I can't wrap my head around the fact that Marcus killed Clarence. And that he tried to kill Jasper, Jax, and me as well. Can you believe how he's deceived everyone for so long?"

Sara nodded. "I am ashamed to say that he had me keeping books for his 'other' business while on the clock for the town. I would never have done it, even though it paid well, and heaven knows we need the money if I'd known what it was. About two weeks ago, I suspected his deals weren't legitimate. Some numbers didn't add up. He told me not to worry, that he'd fix it before tax time. I researched and traced some checks back to a fake account. I wasn't familiar with the entire story, but the business was sketchy enough to convince me I had to stop working for him."

"He sure fooled me," said Jane.

"Dave worked for him, too. That poor guy would do anything for extra money. He had a grudge against Clarence as well since it was his fault that his dad was in the car accident. I think Dave knew more than I did, and when Marcus's goons hounded him for money, he got scared."

Jane nodded. "I know he was scared for Anne's safety as well."

"And for good reason. These guys are professional killers." Sara shivered.

"Jax was the innocent in this entire scheme. He told me Clarence had tracked him down. Found him in an Arizona library and persuaded him to come to Crooked Run. Convinced him he needed to see that justice was done."

"And Jax believes in justice."

Jane continued. "Apparently, Marcus was tired of being blackmailed and threatened to cut off the money supply. I guess Clarence saw Jax as his security blanket. Another person who knew the story."

"I hope Jax pulls out of this," said Sara.

"Me too," said Jane. "But where will he stay if he recovers? I'm sure he has a long road ahead."

"That he will," said Sara. "Rumor has it the Fairchild sisters are reopening their boarding house. I wonder if he could stay with them?"

Jane looked doubtful. "They wouldn't be able to care for an invalid. It's a struggle for them to manage on their own."

"They have that retired Scotland Yard guy. Jasper."

"Jasper is a wonderful person, but I don't think he's that kind of caregiver." Jane sighed. "Let's hope Jax makes it. After that, we can find a home for him."

The double doors to the waiting room swung open, and the doctor approached Jane. "Are you the patient's next of kin?"

"No, but I'm the only one here for him now. Jax was homeless, so I don't know who to contact as his closest relative."

"We should find out. Mr. Porter is in critical condition. However, I have reason to hope he will pull through. Despite being run down, Mr. Porter is basically healthy. He lost a lot of blood, but it was a clean wound. The bullet missed all the major organs."

Both Jane and Sara breathed a sigh of relief.

Chapter 23

"Oh, Jane! What awful luck!" Bethel gushed. Her face revealed feelings that contradicted her words. "Your bass singer is in jail for murder, and both your lead alto and lead soprano have strep. I guess you'll have to give up the choir competition this year."

"I guess you're mistaken," said Jane. "Jasper Reaves is singing bass, and the Fairchild sisters are taking strong antibiotics. They assure me they'll be back in action for the opening round."

Bethel's smile faded. "You're going to put your choir through the rigors of the contest right after all the trauma they suffered at the hands of that imposter?"

"Music is healing, Bethel. We took a vote, and every choir member wants to continue with the competition."

"Well, if you think it's best. But don't lose heart if you don't place this year. Everyone will understand if you're less than your best."

"I appreciate you stopping by, Bethel, but we'll be fine. And it's okay if we don't place. The experience will do us good. Lift our spirits."

Bethel shook her head. "I can't help but admire your spunk, Jane. I wish you well."

Bethel gave a backward wave as she walked down the aisle of the Fellowship Church. True, the Harmony Choir had some significant setbacks over the past few weeks. Still, their willingness—their eagerness—to take part was a tribute to their ability to bounce back after adversity. She turned back to Clarence's music notebook. The man had been an irritable perfectionist, but he had known his music. He'd trained the choir well. They might not place this year, but Jane was sure they'd give it their best.

A disturbance came from the back of the church. The Fairchild sisters. Jane shook her head. They shouldn't be out and about. Why weren't they inside drinking honey and lemon tea and resting their voices?

"Lillie, I tell you, putting a naked Cupid in the cornucopia is in bad taste," said Vada.

"I'll strategically place oak leaves around him. Nobody will know he's there," said her sister.

"If they won't notice, why put him there?" said Emily. "You only want to cause trouble."

"Cupid is a classical expression of love," insisted Lillie. "Trust me, this church needs all the love it can get." Lillie looked up. "Oh, hi Jane. We're bringing in the Thanksgiving decorations. After our streak of bad luck, we need an extra spread of goodwill."

"Ladies, shouldn't you be nursing your sore throats at home?" Jane looked at the motley crew. They were quirky, windswept versions of The Three Graces.

"Jasper whipped us up a supernatural cure," said Emily. The miracle worker trailed behind her, lugging two large buckets of pumpkins and gourds.

"Just bring those up front, dear," said Vada. "We'll put them all around the altar."

"Should he be carrying those heavy buckets? Wasn't he recently discharged from the hospital?" Jasper's left arm was in a sling.

"He said he was fine. Anyway, the pumpkins have dried out. Not much weight to them at all."

"Don't harm my lead bass," said Jane. "Are you ladies up for a rehearsal later this evening?" "We leave in two days for Virginia Beach."

"We'll be there," chorused the Fairchild sisters.

The ladies circled the altar and strewed leaves and pumpkins around the pulpit. Jasper motioned for Jane to follow him to the back of the church. They sat down on a bench near the sound booth.

"Do you reckon Dave and Anne will be at practice this evening?" Jane asked.

"I'm sure. They were at the Latte this morning. Dave seemed so relieved that Marcus was behind bars. He also told me he's getting help with his dad now."

"That's wonderful! Who is helping?" asked Jane.

"Edith from the choir. Dave said she's a retired nurse."

"Wow! I didn't know that. I wonder…" Jane's voice trailed off.

"What do you wonder?" asked Jasper, smiling.

"Oh, nothing. It's only a passing idea. Does Edith live alone? I regret to say that I don't know much about her. I need to get a list of addresses from Rev. Barnard. After this choir competition, I'll set up a regular visitation schedule."

"Edith lives in the apartment Marcus owned. I'm not sure what will happen to the buildings now. I caught wind of the sisters discussing this only yesterday. They were talking about inviting Edith to live with them. They appear to be quite serious about opening the boarding house again."

"I've mulled over some ideas, but they're not going anywhere. So, I guess I'll simply say it. I process things out loud," said Jane.

"Go ahead! I'm always open to your ideas."

"What if Edith moves into the Fairchild house along with Dave's dad," she hesitated, "and Jax? When he gets out of the hospital, of course."

Jasper whistled. "You have been pondering this a lot, haven't you? That move would require a lot of planning, but I'd say that it's worth looking into."

"Do you have any idea what they would charge? I doubt either Mr. Harper or Jax would have a steady income," said Jane.

"We'd have to work through the details, but the sisters would most likely be open to discussing the idea."

"Let's wait until after the competition," said Jane. "We have enough on our plates for the next few days."

***

"Oh, how the mighty have fallen." Chief Smith locked the cell door. "I don't suppose you'll be our guest too long. I think I hear the State Penitentiary calling your name."

Marcus didn't answer. He stared ahead as the door clanged. Smith's footsteps echoed down the hallway. He hadn't planned for his story to end this way. To be defeated by a retired Scotland Yard cop and a choir director was demoralizing. He, Marcus Justice, had beaten all the odds. He'd escaped a criminal past and recreated his identity. For 40 years, he had been a pillar of the community. His life would have continued to roll along without incident. His side business was making all the money he needed—at least, it was until Clarence Jackson got greedy. Now, that same source of income would be just another nail in his coffin. Not only would they try him for murder, but they'd hit him with drug charges, too. Well, not if he could help it. And he was sure he could help it.

The sun was setting, and the room was getting dark. Marcus knew that the cell in the police office was only a temporary spot. As Smith said, they'd be moving him to the state facility in the next day or two. Yeah, Smith knew a lot. But what the chief didn't know was how insecure the cell was. The lock was cheap. And fragile.

He'd wait it out. He'd watch for Smith to go home and make sure Deputy Harris had left for choir rehearsal. And after they were gone, he'd make his escape. Of course, the place had alarms and security cameras. But they hadn't yet had time to change the locks or passcodes. He bet they'd have that on their agenda for tomorrow. But tomorrow was many hours away.

Headlights streamed through the small window in the cell. Chief Smith was leaving. The building was empty. He waited another thirty minutes and then set to work on the lock on the cell door. Ironically, he was the one who bought and installed the jail alarm. The council members insisted on buying the cheapest system possible. Crooked Run was virtually crime-free. Why would they need beefed-up security? They were so smug and self-satisfied. For all they knew, their little cardboard construction was invincible.

If only it were possible to sneak into the hospital and attend to that bothersome vagrant. He found it difficult to accept that he had failed to eliminate Jax with his first attempt. That entire operation was a bust. But this time, he wouldn't fail. This time, he was ready. A pistol rested in the lockbox in his office.

Shutting the cell door behind him, Marcus crept to his office door. His desk was a mess. Smith must have rifled through every paper in the file cabinet. Marcus hadn't planned to get caught, but he was cautious. Certainly, incriminating evidence was everywhere, but it remained concealed. The investigators would have to work for it. He didn't care what they found. He'd be long gone when they were ready to press charges. Granted, he was a little old to start over again, but what choice did he have? He still had his best asset: his sharp, clever brain. He clicked through the passcode on the lockbox and removed the gun. He slipped out the back door of the town office and into the chilly night.

"Going somewhere?"

Marcus froze. In the street lamp's light, he saw the figure of a man. A man who held a gun.

Chapter 24

"How did you guess he'd try to escape?" Chief Smith leaned back in his chair and studied Jasper.

"I wasn't sure he'd try, but I've had enough experience with criminal masterminds to be prepared for any contingency. Since the holding cell was in a building with which Marcus was familiar, I thought he might devise an escape plan. People don't get to his criminal level by not planning ahead. I'm sure Marcus worked through all possibilities before he attempted his escape."

"But he didn't plan for you," said deputy Harris with admiration.

"We'd have picked him up sooner or later. He wouldn't have gotten far," said the Chief.

Harris looked doubtful.

"The state prison won't be as easy to break out of. I suspect they will lock him up for a long time."

Smith grunted. "I reckon you want to run for mayor now."

"Who, me?" Jasper looked surprised. "I'm sure there are laws on your books about foreigners holding public office. Besides, I don't have a green card. I'm still here on a work visa."

"A work visa?" Smith asked. "You really do work for those Fairchild ladies?"

"Yes, I am an official employee of Miss Emily Fairchild."

"I'm sure you have your hands full," said Harris. "I wouldn't want to handle those three."

"Oh, there's no handling to it," said Jasper. "They tell me what to do, and I do it."

"Guess I need to apologize for how I reacted to you when you offered to help with this case. My city buddies give me a rough time because I've had so little experience dealing with crime. I guess I was a bit insecure about leading a murder investigation." Smith looked down at the floor.

"You live in a safe place. That's a positive," said Jasper.

"I'd like to think I can handle anything that might come my way."

"I get it," said Jasper. "And I don't mean to intrude. I wanted to make sure you know I'm here if you ever need a sounding board. I'm always willing to put in my two cents' worth."

Smith stood up and reached to shake Jasper's hand. "Thank you, Mr. Reaves. Jasper. I hope we don't have any more brushes with serious crime. But in looking into Marcus's past, I have found plenty of reasons to indicate he was dealing with a rough crowd. Drug dealers."

Jasper whistled. "Now, that is one group of people we don't want in Crooked Run."

"You're right," said Chief Smith. "And we'll do anything we can to keep them out."

Chapter 25

The day of the contest dawned bright and sunny. Both the Harmony and Trinity Choir arrived at Crooked Run Fellowship early, eager to get started. The shiny red and white Speeddog bus was parked in the circular driveway, the engine humming.

"Jane, you poor thing. You look ragged." Bethel ran to Jane and gave her a quick air hug. "You are all just the bravest for trying out. And after everything you've been through."

"Thank you, Bethel. You're right. We have been through a lot. But, as they say, music soothes the soul. I think this trip will be good for us."

"She looks like an iced animal cracker," muttered Vada, eyeing Bethel's showy pink pantsuit and her yellow hat.

"What's that, dear?" asked Bethel. "You like my outfit?"

"Well, it's bright." Vada put her hand to her forehead as though shading her eyes from a light too bright for mere mortal eyes.

"I like to stand out," said Bethel as she ushered the Harmony choir members to the back of the bus. "I hope you don't mind shifting toward the rear. Several of my choir members suffer from car sickness. Or bus sickness," she giggled.

"With pleasure," murmured Lillie under her breath. "I'll go blind if I stare at that fuchsia and yellow monstrosity for the next six hours."

"Shall we do a sing-along?" asked Bethel, ignoring Lillie's disparaging words. "That will warm our voices up and keep us sharp."

The Fairchild sisters stared at her. "We'll save our voices," said Lillie. "A nap will do me a world of good."

Jasper sat down beside Jane. "Well, Partner in Crime, are you ready for

155

this?"

Jane smiled. "I'm ready to be finished with it all. I think if I ever stop to process the past few weeks, I'll have a nervous breakdown."

"And I thought I might get bored in this small town!"

"I'm hoping for a large dose of boredom in the coming winter months," sighed Jane. "I'd hibernate with the bears if I could."

***

Six hours later, the bus pulled into the performance hall's parking lot. The Centennial Cathedral paid homage to its name. It was a majestic venue with sleek lines and glass facades. The steeple reflected the late fall sun, creating an almost heavenly glow.

Emily, however, was not impressed. "Centennial Cathedral. What kind of name is that? Sounds like the headquarters of a money-hungry TV evangelist."

Jane said, "I understand they built it to mark the church's 100th anniversary. But I agree. The name sounds rather ostentatious."

"I bet the acoustics are good, though," said Brad. He turned to Jasper. "Are you comfortable singing Marcus's part? You haven't had many practices."

Jasper looked at the small group of singers. Someday, he'd tell them about a few musical adventures he'd been part of, but today was not the day. "I'll be okay. You sing extra loud, and I'll follow."

Brad grinned. "We wouldn't be here without you, sir. You lead, and I'll follow."

"I was in the right place at the right time," said Jasper.

"Come on." Emily tapped her cane on the sidewalk. "I am not about to walk up those steps without your help, Jasper."

The line of choir members filing into the building in front of them resembled a meandering rainbow.

"Looks like we're the only emerald green color," said Lillie, looking down her nose at the rusty brown robes the Trinity choir wore.

"Well, no one will accuse us of being gaudy," said Bethel, glaring at Lillie.

"Not until you take off your robe and they see your outfit," Lillie retorted.

Equally impressive as the outside, the inside of the church was breathtaking. The foyer's polished marble floors extended into an aisle leading to the main auditorium. Plush burgundy cushions covered the solid oak pews, while an enormous cornucopia of harvest gatherings adorned the altar.

Lillie whistled. "This place would make the devil sing like an angel."

"He is an angel, sister," said Emily in a loud whisper. "An angel of darkness."

"If you care to be technical," said Lillie, "I'm pretty sure the Good Book refers to him as an angel of light."

"Ladies," said Jane. "Please stop bickering. We need to enter a worshipful spirit to perform our best. We can discuss theology after the contest."

The backstage at the Centennial buzzed.

"Did you see that sound equipment, Jasper?" asked Sara, adjusting the collar of her robe.

"Oh, the possibilities if we had only a fraction of that gear back in Crooked Run," said Brad. "We're going to sound amazing!"

"Don't shake the rafters with that bass voice, Brad. We're all used to singing loudly to compensate for our cheap microphones."

Brad smiled. "I'll make sure the heavens take notice of us tonight. Let's give them a performance to remember."

Meanwhile, Jane huddled with Anne in a corner, reviewing last-minute details. The pianist adjusted her glasses and nodded. "I've got the piano accompaniment down to the last sixteenth note, Jane. We're going to rock this competition."

"You hold us together, Anne. Now, let's show them what Harmony is made of."

A silence fell over the auditorium. The show was about to begin. The organizers had scheduled Crooked Run's Harmony choir to perform third, right before the Trinity choir. They listened as the first two music groups took the stage and poured their hearts into the sacred hymns.

"Wow, they're good!" whispered Jen. "Listen to that complex arrangement of He Shall Lead His Flock!"

"I don't think my hands move that fast," Anne said. "Maybe we're not as good as I thought we were."

"Just remember to smile and breathe! And most important of all, enjoy yourselves!"

The applause from choir number two had died down, and the announcer signaled Jane should bring the Harmony choir on stage.

Anne played the introduction, and their song began. Jane closed her eyes briefly as Sara's soprano soared into the high ceilings. Her voice intertwined with Jasper's resonant bass, creating a dynamic harmony that filled the sacred space. Even Edith's alto was audible above the mingling of voices.

When the song finished, the choir bowed, and the auditorium erupted with applause.

"Well, what did you think, Jane?" asked Vada as soon as they had moved behind the curtain. "My voice cracked a little, but Sara covered me well."

"I'm glad you finally landed on that E-flat, Edith," said Lillie.

Edith blushed.

"There's always room for improvement, friends. But we made Crooked Run Fellowship proud today," said Jane.

They moved to the auditorium to enjoy the rest of the performers.

***

The awards ceremony was a gala event. The church fellowship hall was as large as a banquet room. Crisp white tablecloths covered rows of oval tables. Fine china, polished silverware, and sparkling glassware made the place look like an opulent hotel rather than a church gathering room.

The Harmony choir sat together near the front of the room, as far away from the Trinity choir as possible. The bus ride was all the musical togetherness they could stand.

"Didn't you love it when Bethel almost tripped on the stage?" said Lillie. "I knew those stiletto heels were a bad choice."

"Their entire tenor section sounded like fingernails on a blackboard," said Emily, glancing over at the far corner where the Trinity choir sat.

"Ladies," chided Jane. "This is not the time for petty conversation. We all did well. Let's forget about singing and contests and enjoy this delectable food! Just look at this Caprese Salad; I've never seen so much basil!"

"And the menu said the main course is Filet Mignon with Red Wine Sauce. Can you believe they're serving a wine sauce at a religious gathering?" exclaimed Lillie.

"Jesus turned water into wine. I don't see what's so scandalous about a red wine sauce," Emily smirked.

"Ladies, please," Jane said, "let's try to relax and have a good time."

As the singers finished the last of the Chocolate Lava Cake, the judges made their way to the front of the room with the news. Every contestant was eager to find out which choir would win the European tour.

"Ladies and gentlemen—fellow singers — you have all performed admirably today. Every note, every word, every tune gave glory to God. I believe the praises we lifted up today pleased our Creator.

"Just get on with it!" hissed Emily.

"And now," continued the judge, "the moment you've all been waiting for. The list, please!"

"If he calls for a drum roll, I'm walking out," said Emily.

"Hush, sister! You're not supposed to be here. You're not a member of any choir." Lillie jabbed her elbow into Emily's side.

"First place goes to the Seraphic Sounds for their stunning performance of Lead On, Good Shepherd." A roar of applause sounded through the hall. "We award second place to Voices of Faith for their rendition of All the

Praise, and we present the third place trophy to Spirit Song, who performed a beautiful arrangement of Amen: A Choral Anthem."

Although the Harmony Choir did not place in any of the top three spots, the judges honored them with a newly created award: the Choir that overcame the most adversity.

***

After the awards banquet, the group agreed to return to the hotel and relax for the evening. They were grateful they'd planned to spend the night in Virginia Beach. Nobody wanted to board the Speeddog for another six-hour drive. Who could have imagined that singing would require such energy?

Sara did not look forward to going back to work on Monday. The news about Marcus's capture, escape, and recapture was all over Crooked Run. The phones would ring off the hook. She was also sure folks knew about her unwitting part in the undercover drug dealings. But it was finished. No more covert operations. No more catering to Marcus's whims. If she were honest, she must admit she would miss the extra money. But keeping the books for a shady operation was not worth it. She wanted a job that would make Brayden proud. She relaxed into the deck chair, closed her eyes, and let the cool beach air wash over her.

"Penny for your thoughts."

Sara turned around. Jasper Reaves stood beside her.

"Hello, Jasper."

"I guess I should offer a dollar fifty for your thoughts these days. Inflation."

"More like two dollars!" Sara moved over and patted the seat beside her. "Sit down. It's a lovely evening. Too bad our choir didn't place."

"We got an award. The most resilient musical group. That was something."

"Similar to a participation medal?" Sara laughed. "I'm just glad it's over."

"Yeah, me too." Jasper squinted and twisted his head.

"What do you see?"

"Our hotel brochure says we have an ocean-front view. If you turn your head to the left and look straight up, you'll find a space between those two high-rise buildings. If you squint, you can almost glimpse a line of blue water."

Sara grimaced. "Marcus booked the rooms. He got the cheapest rates possible."

"Well, it's only for a night. What did you think of the contest?"

"You mean the actual singing part or the overall experience?" asked

159

Sara.

"Both."

"I felt disappointed with our performance. We had the potential to do better. But I guess with all the stress and drama that has gone on, we did well enough."

"I agree with you," said Jasper. "By the way, you have a lovely voice."

"That's a nice thing to say. In high school, I wanted to be a professional singer."

"You could have made it. What happened?"

"Life happened. I met Brayden's father, and we fell hard for each other. We were married right out of high school. Then Brayden came along, and I didn't have time to consider returning to school to study music."

"The best-laid plans," said Jasper. "But don't give up on your dream. You're still very young."

Sara sighed. "I appreciate your confidence but will confine my singing career to the Harmony choir. But first, I have to pay the price for working for Marcus. Chief Smith is hopeful that I will fare pretty well. After all, we did what our boss told us to do. I knew he had a shady business on the side, but I honestly didn't suspect he was dealing drugs."

"He is a piece of work," said Jasper. "I can't believe he could live a completely different life with a fake identity. And he pulled it off for so many years."

"And if it weren't for you, he'd still be spreading his poison all over Crooked Run."

"It took a team. I was in the right place at the right time," said Jasper.

"Well, I am so grateful you had the foresight to expect his escape." Sara smiled.

"It was a hunch; that's all." A hunch born of many years of experience, he thought, but he didn't want to bore the young woman with tales of his Scotland Yard days.

Sara stood and stretched. "I'm exhausted. I think I'll turn in for the night. I expect I'll need all the strength I can muster for the next few months."

    ***

Jane felt completely drained; keeping her eyes open was a chore. She hoped Jen and Brad didn't stay out too late. Jan didn't have a room key, and because of all the recent events in Crooked Run, she wasn't comfortable leaving her door unlocked.

She opened a water bottle and walked to the window. The room she shared with Jen was a floor above everyone else. She saw two people basking in the sunset's beauty on the balcony below. Sara and Jasper. A sudden pang akin to jealousy washed over her. She scolded herself. Jasper was free to hang out with whomever he wished.

She moved away from the window and took out her worn copy of Mere Christianity. Another evening with C.S. Lewis.

***

"It's best if we take a break from seeing each other for a while," said Anne. "I still have a lot to process, and you have some decisions to make." The ocean breeze turned chilly after the sun had set. She and Dave were the last two people on the deck.

Dave dropped his head into his hands and sighed. "I don't think I have any decisions left to make. Marcus is in jail, so I can't work for him anymore."

"Is that the only reason you're changing? You're sorry you got caught?"

"No, I told you. I'm turning over a new leaf. I don't know how I'll support Dad and myself, but whatever means I find, it will be legal."

"Can you ask for a raise?"

"No. Working for the town is different from working at a private company. You can't ask for more money without going through all the proper channels."

"Well, we both have stuff to work on. And my divorce isn't final yet. Not that there's any chance of Tom and I getting back together. I don't want to jump from one relationship to another."

"So I'm a rebound?" Dave looked hurt.

"No, not at all. And I'm not giving up on us. We both need some space."

"A polite way of breaking up with me. I get it."

"If that's how you insist on seeing it, then yes, I'm breaking up with you."

They fell into an uncomfortable stillness as they listened to the distant sound of crashing waves.

Dave's phone jingled. He'd almost turned it off when he came out to sit with Anne. But in the back of his mind, he still expected an emergency call about his dad. The healthcare worker who stayed with the elder Harper man during Dave's absence was competent, and Dave was sure she was up for any challenge. Still, he worried.

He glanced at the screen. "It's Lillie Fairchild. I should probably take it."

"Of course," said Anne, walking toward the door. "We can talk more on the way home. I'll stay in Edith's room tonight."

***

The Harmony choir joined the Trinity choir in a sing-along on the journey back to Crooked Run. Trinity had tied for fourth place with a

161

small church choir from Southwest Virginia. Bethel looked disappointed when the judge announced the final decision but appeared pleased with the trophy.

"I've already picked the music for next year," she told Jane. "We're going to practice right after the Christmas Pageant. What are your plans for the upcoming contest? Will you be leading again?"

"Bethel, we just finished this year. Let me rest from the past several weeks before I consider next year."

Bethel clicked her tongue. "Okay, but don't forget, we'll be ahead of you."

"That's fine, Bethel. Now, if you'll excuse me, I need to talk with the Fairchild sisters." Jane walked down the aisle, struggling to keep her balance as the bus hit a rough patch in the road. She might fall flat, but at least she'd be away from Bethel Green.

Jane winced as she heard Bethel's voice over the noise of the bus. "Let's sing Michael Row Your Boat Ashore. All together now. Four-part harmony." She pulled out a pitch pipe and blew the starting note.

Chapter 26

"Today's the day!" Vada opened the curtains and let the late November sun shine through the living room. The air was frosty, and the forecast called for snow later in the week. But today was gorgeous, a perfect omen for new beginnings.

"I feel like we've forgotten something important." Lillie plopped her checklist down on the table. "But I guess all we had to do was get the rooms ready and fill the pantry."

"Emily assured me she and Jasper took care of the food," said Vada, "although I suspect she didn't use the list I gave her."

"What makes you say that?" Lillie asked as she sat down next to the fireplace.

"For starters, it's still on the table," Vada sighed and sat beside her sister. "We made the right decision when we talked with Home Health before we spent money on a lift chair. I'm glad so much of the furniture we need is available for rent. And for a lot less money than we'd spend if we had to buy it."

"Are we taking on more than we can handle, Vada? We're not spring chickens ourselves." Lillie picked up Charcoal and rubbed her silky black fur. "Sometimes I'd like to grow old sitting by the fire with my knitting and cat." Charcoal gave a sharp meow as though confirming it was a good idea. "But then, I remember how much fun we had with the boarding house. How many people we met and the lives we touched."

Vada looked thoughtful. "I hope we can keep the place open for a long time. I'm glad we hired Edith as a home health nurse. I'm sorry she lost her place when Marcus's apartment building went on the market, but it will be nice to have her here."

"Any idea when they'll release Jax from the hospital?"

"Not for a while, according to Jane. The poor man needs to rest and build up his strength."

"I never believed we could persuade Mr. Harper to stay with us." Lillie stood to straighten a stack of kindling wood, dropping a disgruntled Charcoal to the floor. "He's a proud man. He didn't want to accept what he called 'charity.'"

"He can pay what he can afford," said Vada. "We're not hurting for money. I'm happy with the sliding scale Sara created for us."

"I'm glad Dave decided to stay here with his dad for the weekend. Edith can't come until Monday. Listen! I think I hear a car in the driveway. Surely the Harpers aren't here already."

The doorbell rang as Vada moved to look out the window. Jane stood on the porch, holding a bouquet of dried flowers.

"Why, Jane! I'm so glad you stopped by!"

"I wouldn't miss your big day for the world! Are you all set?"

"I hope so." Vada looked around the cozy parlor. "Come in and sit with us. We're waiting for Dave and his father. Lillie, find a vase for this lovely bouquet."

Jane hung her jacket on the coat rack by the door. "We've had quite an eventful autumn, haven't we? It'll be a while before I've processed it all."

"That's the understatement of the year," agreed Lillie. "But I'm glad it all ended well."

"It did…eventually," agreed Jane. "Rev. Barnard has asked me to take over this year's Christmas pageant. He says all that practice time is too much for him. I think some older children are giving him a hard time."

"In my experience, it's been the parents who are the worst. Every dad wants his daughter to be Mary, and every mama wants a Joseph in the family. There would have to be at least twenty holy families to suit everybody." Lillie shook her head at the folly.

"You're jumping from one crazy schedule to the next. Christmas is only a few weeks away. And what about the choir cantata? We started practicing right before Clarence decided we'd enter the choir competition." Vada looked concerned. "We haven't sung a note of the carols since then."

"I hope Jasper will consider leading the cantata. I can't handle adults and children both." Jane sighed. "But I'm looking forward to a long winter's rest after the first of the year."

"I guess we'll also have to elect a new mayor," said Vada. "I don't have any idea who might be qualified to run. What about you, Jane?"

Jane laughed. "One responsibility at a time, Vada. Some people in town have enough trouble accepting me as a spiritual leader. There would be a riot if I led the town as well."

"Too bad Jasper isn't eligible to take office. He would make a strong town leader," said Emily.

"I'm sure the council will fill the gap," said Lillie. "The town manager will be back next week. Won't he be surprised at all that's happened while he was gone? I bet he'll never go on vacation again!"

"Yes, it'll all work out," said Emily. "Dave and his father should be here any minute. Are you ready to be a boarding house proprietor again, Vada?"

"I believe I am," said Vada, smiling.

Jane walked to the back porch to direct the Harpers to the ramp when they arrived. Despite the cool temperatures, the sun carried a comforting warmth, and Jane tilted her face toward the light.

She had learned from Jasper that Dave and Sara would go on trial for their role in Marcus's underground drug dealing. Some rumors connected Dave with missing church money as well. The town council had already agreed that Sarah should keep her job as a secretary but with a slight twist. She would be secretary for the town, not for the new mayor. The town position would mean a significant pay increase.

Anne had told Jane that she and Dave were going to part ways. At least for a time. That was likely for the best. They had gotten off to a bumpy start. Maybe they could salvage their relationship, but some space apart would help.

Jasper had volunteered to continue co-directing the Harmony choir with her if she was interested in leading. At some point, she hoped he would take it over. She wanted to concentrate more on her duties as assistant pastor of Crooked Run Fellowship. She knew some members still resented her presence. Their opinions may change. Maybe they wouldn't. But now, for the first time since moving to Crooked Run, she was sure she was where she was supposed to be.

She heard Dave's truck rumbling up the road. She was so glad the young man would get some relief from caregiving. The Fairchild sisters had a renewed purpose. The old Victorian house would again be abuzz with activity. They were already talking about building a sunporch and adding another bedroom. Their stamina and positive outlook for the future impressed Jane. Most people in their seventies were retired. But the Fairchild sisters were in the early stages of a new career. She should take inspiration from that.

"This way," she called as Dave pulled into the driveway. "Jasper will bring a wheelchair to the ramp."

The adventure had begun.

Epilogue

Clarence's last word

He'd never liked the sound of flutes, but it was the only instrument he could play in this strange middle land. He sat under an evergreen tree in the Crooked Run woods behind the Rev. Jane Cartwright's house. The icy wind whistled through the trees as snow fell. The woods had its own special music.

Nature singing, humming, and clapping in time to an eternal tune. He was glad he'd landed in Crooked Run. He could still monitor things. Make sure the Harmony choir stayed in tune. He hoped Jane would decide to be the official choir director. Of course, she didn't measure up to his precise standards, but who could? He chuckled. He'd have loved to have been present for that choir competition.

He didn't know the rules of his new existence yet. Maybe in time, he could whisper some directions into Jane's ear. She could excel as a musician with proper guidance—anything to beat that pompous Bethel Green.

The choir would practice for the Christmas cantata soon. He may slip in a flute note occasionally without causing too much havoc. He thought the only rule he had to observe was to stay out of sight. Not that it would be a problem. He couldn't even see himself yet. That vision would come in time, he was sure. For now, he'd just enjoy floating around and keeping an eye on things. He raised his flute to his lips and played a soulful melody–inaudible to most ears and easily mistaken for the wind.

Bio

Tammy Fulk Cullers is a Jill-of-all-trades and hopes to (one day) master one. She is a middle school English teacher by day and a mystery writer by night. She also morphs into a newspaper publisher the last week of every month. Her future goals include learning to do cryptic crossword puzzles, owning a bookstore, and (eventually) becoming Jane Marple.

She has co-written three local history books and was part of a trio-of cozy mystery writers and published three books under the name Mary Fulk Larson

If you enjoyed your visit to Crooked Run, please
leave a review on Amazon!

If you'd like to keep up with what's happening in
Crooked Run, subscribe to the newsletter! Visit the
website
www.crookedrunmysteries.com for more
information.

Email me at
mysterymail@crookedrunmysteries.com

www.ingramcontent.com/pod-product-compliance
Lightning Source LLC
Chambersburg PA
CBHW032014170626
46807CB00006B/2802